Four Regency Stories

Kisses
& Rogues

Anthea Lawson

Kisses & Rogues print anthology copyright 2012 Anthea Lawson. The Piano Tutor originally published in The Mammoth Book of Regency Romance, Running Press, July 2010.

Cover photo by hamara. Used from fotolia with licensed permission.

Discover more Anthea Lawson at anthealawson.com
(Anthea also writes Young Adult fantasy as Anthea Sharp—www.antheasharp.com)

This collection is licensed for your personal enjoyment only. Thank you for respecting the hard work of this author. To obtain permission to excerpt portions of the text, other than for review purposes, please contact the author at anthea@anthealawson.com.

All characters and events in these stories are fictional, and figments of the author's imagination.

QUALITY CONTROL: Producing error-free books is a priority. If you find a typo or formatting problem, send a note to anthea@anthealawson.com so it can be corrected.

ISBN – 13: 978-1479333134

Table of Contents

FIVE WICKED KISSES – 3
To pay off her father's debt, Juliana Tate must accept five kisses from the Earl of Eastbrook... but she never suspects how delicious each kiss will be.

MAID FOR SCANDAL – 55
Miss Anna Harcourt disguises herself as a maid to be near the man she thinks she loves, but little does she know how far this charade will lead her ... or how close to scandal.

THE PIANO TUTOR – 107
Encouraged by her scandalous friend to take a lover, Lady Diana Waverly finds that the new piano tutor is more than he seems — especially when it comes to passion.

TO WED THE EARL – 135
Miss Miranda Price detests her neighbor Edward Havens, the rakish Earl of Edgerton—but when he catches her breaking into his library at midnight, secrets are revealed that will change the course of their lives... forever.

Anthea Lawson

Five Wicked Kisses

~CHAPTER ONE~

"**H**e's watching you."

Juliana Tate did not need to turn around to know who her friend Henrietta was referring to. There was, and had only ever been, one *he*.

Waves of heat raced just under her skin, and her heart tumbled abruptly in her chest. Their corner of the ballroom, chosen for its seclusion, was suddenly crowded with the hum of conversation and bright spikes of laughter.

She flipped open her lace-edged fan and wafted air across her cheeks. There could be no hint of reaction, no sign that the arrival of Robert Pembroke, the new Earl of Eastbrook, affected her.

Since she had come up to London, she had seen him on precisely three occasions—and each time had done her utmost stay as far away as possible.

"You told me he was not invited." Her voice wavered, only the tiniest bit, but she knew her friend heard. "Hen, I depend upon you completely. You're the only one who knows."

Henrietta made an apologetic face. "He wasn't supposed

to be here. But it's hardly the first time the Earl of Eastbrook has paid no heed to the social niceties. You know what they say about him."

Since ascending to the title six months ago, Robert had taken to life in London with a vengeance. According to the gossips, he had cut a wide swath through the ladies, leaving words like *seducer* and *scoundrel* in his wake. Juliana could well believe it.

Robert had always been handsome enough to break hearts, with his strong jaw, keen amber eyes, and dark hair shot through with glints of fire. Not to mention a sharp mind and stubborn temper.

Once, she would have ascribed kindness and a thoughtful heart to him as well—but it seemed all traces of that man were gone. No doubt he was pleased to bring so many ladies of the *ton* to their knees, after years of being treated as unworthy—a shabby country cousin.

And Juliana had been the worst offender.

She plied her fan harder, trying to wave away the bitter memory. The past was done. All she could do now was move forward into an increasingly precarious future.

"Is he still looking?" she asked. It would be safe to turn around if that penetrating amber gaze were focused elsewhere.

"His attention seems to have moved to Miss Snelling's bosoms. And there is so very much there to admire." Henrietta gave a disapproving sniff. "If her gown were any lower she might as well proclaim herself a melon-seller and be done."

"At least she *has* something to reveal."

Juliana could not help a quick glance down at her own, modest, blue gown. She had turned the seams and added new ribbons, but feared it was sadly evident she was at least two seasons out of date.

"Tsk." Henrietta took her by the arm. "It's hardly your fault you don't have the newest fashions. You cut a lovely enough figure despite it. Heavens knows I've envied your hair for simply ages. It's pure gold."

"A pity it's not actual gold. Though I suppose I could sell it." Things were certainly becoming desperate enough.

"No!" Henrietta gasped. "Promise me you won't."

Juliana raised a hand to her hair, a gently curling wealth of honey-colored locks that fell to her hips when unbound. It was her one vanity, though dark hair was currently in fashion. As were voluptuous figures—which made her quest to find a wealthy husband more difficult. But Henrietta had assured her that she could snare a suitor within a fortnight, if she applied herself.

"Look, there's my aunt peering into the corners," Henrietta said, "No doubt she's wondering where her changes have gone off to. Come along—but keep a watch out for Viscount Wrenforth. He's a likely prospect for you."

"The viscount was very pleasant to me at the Cotteridge's musicale," Juliana said.

"Excellent! He has a fine fortune, and is not *too* ill-favored to look upon. If one disregards the nose."

Juliana nodded. She had no time to lose. The debts were mounting, and there was almost nothing left for her to sell, her hair notwithstanding. Her jewelry now consisted of the strand of pearls about her neck and a single bracelet. The walls of her suite were entirely bare of paintings, though she could not bring herself to sell her books. Yet.

The silver would have to be next, and it would become

obvious that she wasn't simply selling her own belongings for a bit of extra pin money.

Once Society heard of her family's utter destitution, no one would want to marry her. She must be firmly engaged before that happened.

Letting out a quiet breath, she went with Henrietta, careful not to glance toward the ballroom doors. She could not bear to see Robert surrounded by the shimmer of colorful gowns and even more brilliant smiles, knowing she had long ago forfeited her place there.

***

Robert Pembroke watched as the slender figure in the blue gown moved out of sight—not that any of the ladies buzzing around him could tell where his attention was fixed. To all but the keenest observer, his interest appeared to be upon their laughing flirtations.

He could have his pick of the dashing widows and adventurous females. Since becoming the Earl of Eastbrook, he had never wanted for company in his bed. But tonight he would not choose any of the lovelies to dally with, despite their obviously-displayed charms.

No. His thoughts were on one woman alone—a woman with hair like sunlight and the lithe body of a nymph. A woman he had once thought he loved, until she had so cruelly broken his heart.

He had waited four long years to claim revenge on Juliana Tate. Tomorrow, his retribution would begin.

~CHAPTER TWO~

"Miss Juliana, you have a caller. I have put him in the salon." The butler bowed and presented her the salver with a thick vellum card centered upon it.

Oh no. She did not need to pick it up to read the broad script. *Robert Pembroke, Earl of Eastbrook.*

Her lungs tightened and a tingle of nerves coursed up her spine. Robert. Here. In the parlor downstairs.

"Did he give you a reason for his visit? Is he here to see father?"

"He specifically asked for you, mistress."

Juliana drew in a steadying breath. "Well, then."

She raised a hand to her hair, and quashed the foolish urge to change into a better gown. There *were* no better gowns, not since father had gambled away all of their money.

It was fashionable to keep callers waiting, but she preferred to face her problems head-on. She went downstairs, passing the silent study where Father sequestered himself. He emerged only at suppertime, and sometimes not even then. It was how he had always dealt with problems, by ignoring them—though the nature of their troubles was more severe, of late.

Pausing before the parlor, Juliana smoothed her hair one last time, then pushed open the door.

The room seemed suddenly very small with Robert in it, a tall, dark-haired force of nature. She could not help but stare at him, the face she kept in her memory—chiseled cheekbones and mobile lips, hair on the long side of fashionable, and eyes lit with golden fire.

"Miss Tate." He was before her in two steps.

Before she could think to move away, he took her hand and bowed. His grip was firm and insistent.

She felt her pulse race as his attention traveled slowly over her body. His gaze lingered at her legs, her chest, her throat—where she could feel her pulse beating wildly—before he lifted his eyes to her face again.

"You are looking well." The dark promise in his voice shot a tingle up her spine.

Rake. Scoundrel. The words echoed through her body and she felt reckless heat rise in her cheeks. Was this truly the same Robert she had stolen kisses with in the apple orchard, four spring-times ago? Had becoming an earl changed him that much?

She pulled her hand out of his grasp. "Why are you here?"

It was altogether blunt of her, but she could not maintain her composure long enough to play the formal hostess with him. The only thing to do was discover what he wanted, quickly, and send him on his way.

She felt as though she were balanced on a swaying bridge over a chasm. To either side lay dangerous emotions—love, despair. One misstep and she would plunge over the edge.

"So abrupt, Juliana."

The sound of her name on his tongue made her dizzy with longing, with regret. She swallowed. "Would you prefer I call you *my lord* and offer you tea? I'm afraid I cannot."

He gave her a hard look. "I'm glad to see the years haven't changed how you feel about me."

"They have not."

She let her gaze slip from his. He would think she meant disdain, but she had never hated him. Never.

"My condolences on the loss of your mother." His voice was not particularly sympathetic. "You were in mourning for her a rather long time."

Did he suspect her mother's hand in what had happened? He had never liked Lady Tate—and the dislike had been mutual. In truth, her mother had detested young Robert Pembroke. Nearly as much as she had hated her own children.

"Yes," Juliana said. "Father insisted on two years of the black."

Two years of formal mourning. At least the terrible misery of living with her mother had ended. Coming up to London this last month had been almost worse, however, once she had realized the desperate state of their affairs.

"Now you're out of mourning," Robert said, "and enjoying life in Town, I see."

"Not as much as you seem to be."

He leaned forward, with a twist to his lips—those sensuous lips that sent the ladies of the *ton* swooning. Juliana resolved not to think of his mouth.

"Indeed, I'm enjoying London," he said. "Being an earl has its advantages. In fact, I'm here to discuss one of those advantages with you."

Her breath caught in her throat. Was he here to suggest something scandalous?

"I'm sure I don't grasp your meaning," she said.

"Don't you?" He tilted one eyebrow up. "Your father seems to have gotten himself into a bit of trouble at the gaming tables. However, as we're such long-standing acquaintances, I took it upon myself to help."

"What has father done now?" She reached for the back of the settee, hoping Robert could not see her hands tremble. "What have *you* done?"

"You'll be relieved to hear that I've bought up his notes and paid off the creditors." He smiled, without a trace of warmth. "Your father's debts now belong to me."

"What?" Shock rippled through her.

This was dreadful. To have Robert holding such power over them, after what she had done…

He captured her eyes with his own, and his expression sharpened to something predatory. Juliana felt like a wild doe cornered by a hunter. The beating of her heart threatened to drown out all other sound.

"I've spoken with your father," Robert said. "He has agreed that *you* can redeem the debt from me. For a small consideration."

"And what might that consideration be?" Juliana's chest tightened.

She would be ruined, utterly, if she became his mistress. It was a terrifying, exhilarating thought, and she thrust it to the back of her mind.

"I will hand over your father's notes, to dispose of as you like," he said. "After I take payment from you… of five kisses."

She drew in a sharp breath. It was not, after all what she had feared. What she had secretly hoped for. But of course, her father would never have consented to such a thing. Thank goodness her brother was safely away at school. She did not want him to know anything of this situation. He would only do something foolish, like challenge Robert to a duel.

"Five kisses? How very forward of you, sir."

"Ah, Juliana. It is far less than I could have asked. Those debts represent a considerable sum."

It was true. Five kisses was a paltry payment, even considering their reduced circumstances.

Was it possible Robert still cared for her, even after she had turned him away so cruelly? Had her hateful words faded in his memory?

She searched his expression, but there was no softness there, none of the eager yearning they had shared. No, she would be a fool to think that he had forgiven her.

"Why?" The word came out nearly a whisper.

"Because I can." His voice was hard.

"So, I'm just another bauble the earl can buy? A trinket to be played with and then discarded when you are done?"

The thought burned. He didn't even want her for a mistress, he merely wanted to toy with her, like a cat with a mouse under its paw. There was no warmth of sentiment in him. He only wanted revenge.

"Do you deserve better?" His gaze bored into hers. "After heaping such scorn upon me, do you think I'd come to pay you court now?"

"My mother—"

"I didn't see her standing with a pistol at your back that day, making you say those words. You seemed convinced enough that I was unworthy of you. How did you put it? Ah yes… you said I was *no better than the dirt under your feet.*"

She dropped her gaze to the carpet.

How many nights had she lain wakeful in bed with shame burning through her? She had written to him, dozens of apologies and explanations—had tried to post the letters, but her mother had always intercepted them. The consequence of seeing her younger brother punished for her disobedience had put a stop to her efforts. But she still composed messages to Robert in her heart.

"I'm sorry," she said. The words came out nearly a whisper. "It was wrong of me."

"Juliana." He spoke her name like a cold stone. "Do you expect me to believe you feel remorse? You think that, now I'm the Earl of Eastbrook, all should be forgiven between us?"

"It's not because of that!" She lifted her head and met his gaze directly. "I don't care whether you hold a title."

It had been her mother who had cared—strongly enough to force Juliana to break all ties with Robert.

"What a remarkable liar you are." The coolness of his expression did not change. "Let's return to the matter at hand. Your debt to me."

She wrapped her arms about herself. It was clear he would never forgive her.

"I don't see why you'd even want to collect the debt in this manner, since you find me so contemptible. Can't I give you some other payment?" Though what, she couldn't imagine.

"Contemptible, but still beautiful." He reached out and ghosted a touch along the side of her face. "They call you the Ice Maiden, did you know that?"

She shook her head. Perhaps her friend Henrietta had heard, but spared her the knowledge.

Would she even be able to find a suitor, with that name shackling her? She could feel all her plans collapsing. Nothing had ever come out right. Her past, and her future, lay in tumbled ruins at her feet.

What more damage could five kisses do?

"Very well," she said. "I will pay what you ask."

"Good." A slow smile spread the corners of his mouth. "Now, come sit down."

"I really don't—"

"Come." He took her elbow and steered her around the settee.

She perched on the edge, and he sat beside her, too close for any kind of comfort. She remembered kissing him—she dreamed of kissing him. Even if he no longer cared for her, it would not be dreadful.

Ah, if only she were the Ice Maiden in truth—cold and unfeeling. Instead her heart was as vulnerable as a new blossom, in danger of withering under the blight of Robert's disdain.

"I suppose…we had best begin," she said, holding herself stiffly away from him.

Soonest begun, soonest done, her old governess used to say. Juliana closed her eyes. It was too much to hope that he would simply kiss her cheek, but she tilted her head toward him nonetheless.

His low chuckle made her open her eyes. He had not moved, except to extend one arm along the back of the settee. Despite his laughter, his expression was calculating.

"It's not as simple as you seem to think, Juliana. Let me explain exactly how you will fulfill this debt."

"What explanation do five kisses require? Take them and be done!"

His nearness was unbearable. She wanted to fling herself into his arms. She wanted to take to her heels and slam every door between them.

"No," he said. "Each kiss will require a separate visit. I'll take my first payment today, and call upon you the next four Thursday afternoons to claim the remainder."

"I hardly think—"

"You agreed." He held her gaze. Flecks of amber burned in his eyes.

There was nothing she could say to that. She was entirely at his mercy. Her lips parted, and his eyes shifted to her mouth. After a heartbeat, he shook his head.

"Give me your hand," he said.

"My hand?"

"Don't look so surprised. I told you we'll continue under my terms. I choose the placement of these most-expensive kisses."

She should not have agreed without determining what, exactly, Robert had been planning. But even had she known, refusal would have still been impossible. He had neatly trapped her.

"Placement of the kisses?"

"Yes." His gaze smoldered. "There are so many places on your body I could put my mouth. Five is hardly enough to make a beginning."

His words were so full of wickedness she burned from hearing them. She stared at him, her heart pounding.

"Your hand," he said again.

Slowly, Juliana extended her arm. He caught her hand, holding it palm-up. Keeping his gaze locked on hers, he set the fingers of his other hand at her wrist. Then, with exquisite slowness, he drew his fingers down. The movement sent sparks flickering along her nerves. His caress continued on to the warm hollow of her palm, his fingers drawing little circles that sizzled through her entire body.

"Is this necessary?" Her voice was treacherously unsteady. "I thought you were going to kiss my hand, not tickle it."

"Oh, I shall."

He turned her hand over, his grip warm and inescapable. Bending his head, he brought the back of her hand up to his mouth. His lips were firm, and softer than she had expected, warm against her skin. Before she could adjust to the sensation, he flicked his tongue out, and she stifled a gasp.

Where his lips were warm, his tongue was hot. He parted his mouth, his tongue echoing the circling of his fingers, so that her whole hand was engulfed in swirling fire. She swayed back against the cushions, and he glanced up, satisfaction gleaming in his golden eyes.

It took her a moment to find her voice. "Are you quite finished, sir?"

"No." He turned her hand over, cupping it with his own. "Shall I read your fortune?"

"I have no fortune, as you are well aware."

"You have a cruel past, though." For a moment something almost wistful flashed across his face. Then his expression hardened. "And you will pay for it, lovely Juliana."

"I have paid enough, today." She tried to pull her hand away.

"I think not." He kept her hand, and truly, half of her did not want him to release her.

No matter their turbulent past, this had not changed— her body yearned for him in ways she could scarcely understand.

Once again, he lowered his mouth to her skin. The heat of his tongue in the palm of her hand was astonishing, and incredibly intimate. He ravished her now, lacing his fingers through hers and spreading her hand wide, slipping his tongue in and out between her parted fingers.

The tips of her breasts tightened, and sensations she could not name swirled through her—heat and a curious discomfort. Despite her efforts at control, she knew he heard her breathing grow unsteady. She felt as though her entire being was there, throbbing in the center of her palm.

"That… was two kisses," she managed when he finally raised his head.

"No—merely the continuation of a kiss to your hand," he said. He folded her fingers over her palm.

"But…" She gazed into his eyes, seeing no room for argument. Once his mind was made up, there was no swaying him.

"Remember," he said. "I will return on Thursday."

She nodded, then cleared her throat. "The butler will see you out."

She did not trust herself to remain steady on her legs. Not with the aftermath of his kiss storming through her, the tangles of regret and desire knotted about her heart.

"Farewell." He gave the word an ironic twist as he rose and sketched her a bow. He did not look back, and the parlor door swung closed behind him.

Once she was certain he was gone, Juliana slowly opened her hand, as though something fragile and impossible rested in her palm. Robert's kiss, though it was not a lover's kiss.

She would pay a thousand times over for what she had done. If she had thought her life unbearable four years ago, after she had obeyed her mother and turned him away, how much worse would it be now?

To see him, to kiss him, and feel her heart breaking a little more each time. It was clear now why he had taken up Father's debts. It was to punish her. By the time the Earl of Eastbrook was finished taking his payment, their fortune would be restored.

And she would be reduced to nothing.

***

Robert leaned back against the cushioned seats of his carriage, and smiled. That had gone very well, indeed. He'd been prepared for more opposition, but the quickness of Juliana's capitulation was a testament to how perfectly he had played his hand. There was nothing she could do but submit.

The first kiss had affected her just as he had planned. Though she had tried to conceal her reaction, he had been gratified to see how her body betrayed her—her rapid heartbeat, her parted lips. It was only a short distance from arousal to desire, from desire to obsession. He would not call it *love*, that bitter word that curdled in his mouth.

Women and raw youths preferred to paint over the starkness of overwhelming passion, calling it by sweeter, more sentimental terms. But he knew that beneath the rosy haze lay a harder truth. Love did not exist.

He'd learned that lesson. Juliana would, too.

Juliana Tate. Damn, but she was still beautiful, with hair that could make any man yearn to sin. His fingers tingled at the thought of unpinning it, seeing those honeyed waves cascading over her shoulders and down her back. The fantasy of Juliana clothed only in the golden veil of her hair was delectable.

The door of the carriage swung open, a waft of cool spring air interrupting his carnal imaginings.

"My lord," the footman said, setting the steps.

Robert nodded his thanks. Before him rose the imposing façade of the Earl of Eastbrook's town house. His house. He took little pleasure in it—the death of a good man had brought him here. The title and wealth were simply the means to an end. Juliana's downfall.

After she had so cruelly thrust him from her life, it had taken the better part of a year to mend his shattered heart. That year had changed him from a dreamy-eyed youth to a man. He had learned that women lusted for him, and he had honed that power. Not until his cousin had died, leaving him the title, had he begun to think he could claim revenge on Miss Juliana Tate.

Her apology that afternoon had been unexpected. Not genuine, of course—he'd be an utter fool to believe that. Still, he'd thought it would take her longer, by the third kiss perhaps, to offer a show of remorse.

Of course, it was on account of his new title. She'd inherited her mother's grasping nature. Robert stalked up the stairs, not pausing as the butler opened the door. He made his way to the dark-paneled study. A fire burned on the hearth, warding the spring chill from the air.

One of the maids had brought in a spray of apple blossoms. The sight kindled an icy rage within him. Snatching the white-petaled boughs from their vase, he threw them onto the coals. They hissed and smoked and then, at last, burst into flame.

Just as he had burned out the memory of Juliana, white petals caught in her hair, laughing in the apple orchard.

He would bring her low, make her suffer as he had suffered, and then he would be free. Only four kisses stood between him and the future.

~CHAPTER THREE~

"Miss Tate is expecting you, my lord," the butler said to Robert one week later, taking his hat and gloves.

The man led him to the same room as before, a parlor with striped wallpaper and a decided lack of ornamentation. Juliana was standing behind the settee, her arms folded at her waist. She was wearing the same drab dress as last time.

Did she think to put him off with unattractive clothing? Her hair spoiled the intent, however. The honeyed strands were twisted into an awkward coil at the back of her head. His fingers itched with the desire to pull her hairpins out and let that golden cascade tumble freely down.

"Good afternoon," he said.

"My lord."

She made no other concession to his title, no dip of a curtsy, not even an inclination of her head. So proud and intractable. But he would bring her to her knees—figuratively speaking.

When he rounded the settee, she began to move away.

"I refuse to chase you about the room, Juliana," he said, catching her arm. "Stand still."

She swallowed, and he could see her pulse fluttering at her throat. Despite her icy demeanor, she was not unmoved by him. He intended to unsettle her even more.

"Very well." She tilted her cheek to him, as she had done before. "Kiss me and take your leave."

"Dear Juliana." He slid his hand down to the curve of her

waist. "I told you, it's not that simple. Turn around."

He placed his other hand on her other hip, and rotated her until she stood with her back to him.

"Really, sir." She tried to take a step away, but he held her firmly in place. "I don't see -"

"My kisses, to take as I please. As we agreed."

She would see soon enough. He felt a smile curve his lips.

A shiver went through her—he felt it beneath his palms where they rested on the sweet curve of her waist. Slowly, he pulled her back until their bodies were nearly touching. Awareness thrummed through him. A delicious, scant inch of space separated them—the anticipation of touch, preceding the actual moment.

The pale skin of her neck looked smooth as cream satin. He could hardly wait to taste it.

He bent his head, inhaling the scent of orange-flower water drifting up from her hair. Slowly, so that she could feel the heat of his breath, he dropped his lips to hover at the delicate indentation of her nape. Feather-light, he brushed his mouth across her skin. Her stifled gasp made heat flare up in him.

Pressing his lips more firmly to her neck, he nibbled his way to just beneath her ear. Her pulse beat wildly beneath his mouth, though the rest of her remained still as glass.

"Delicious," he whispered.

He raised one hand and pulled gently at the neckline of her dress, exposing her collarbone. Just there, a tracing of the tongue, hot and smooth against her skin. He swirled delicate circles back up toward her ear, and another tremble ran through her.

It did not take long for him to locate the hairpins restraining the glorious mass of her hair. He pulled them out, one by one, and let them land, unheeded, on the carpet. All the while, his lips mapped the arch and curve of her lovely neck.

One strand of hair came free, landing on her shoulder. Her hand flew to the back of her head, but it was too late. Robert pulled out the last pin, and her hair tumbled down in all its golden glory.

She whipped around, her blue eyes hot, her face flushed. "How dare you!"

"What?" He kept his tone light, amused, though the sight of her arousal made a dark tide stir inside him. "I can ravish your neck, but woe betide any man who touches your hair?"

It lay over her shoulder, gleaming like sunlight. He reached for it, he couldn't help himself, and ran his fingers through the soft waves.

Narrow-eyed, she pulled her hair out of his grasp.

"Kisses are one thing," she said, "but I did not give you leave to wreak havoc on my coiffure."

"You prefer to leave that to your lady's maid? She's doing a terrible job of it, I must say. That style doesn't suit you."

"It's none of your concern." Juliana tossed her hair back behind her shoulders. "You've collected your payment for the day, my lord. Now I must bid you farewell."

She had always been beautiful when in a temper. Not that her beauty was any excuse for her past behavior. Still, he enjoyed cracking the façade of the Ice Maiden.

Knowing it would unsettle her, he went down on one knee and swept up the errant hairpins scattered on the carpet. He glanced up and gave her his scoundrel's smile.

"Shall I re-pin it for you?"

"No!" She took a step back, then held out her hand. "My hairpins, if you please."

He rose and considered the bits of metal in his hand. "Perhaps I'll keep them."

Her eyes widened, a flash of something like desperation moving through them. "Give them back. Please." The last word was strained.

Was she really so destitute, that she could not afford to replace a handful of hairpins? He thought back to the magnitude of her father's debts. Well, perhaps she was. And she deserved it.

Truly? a voice inside him whispered, *she deserves to be penniless and afraid?*

"Here." He thrust the hairpins at her, then spun on his heel and stalked out of the room.

Damn it.

Juliana was cold and cruel. She deserved no sympathy from him.

None whatsoever.

~CHAPTER FOUR~

Thursdays shadowed Juliana's entire month. Two had passed, and on the whole, she wanted the next to never come. Yet late at night, while memory kept her wakeful, she wished the days would hasten forward.

If only her mother had not been so cruel, so fixed upon the importance of Juliana wedding a title. Then she and Robert might have married—and she would now be a countess. The irony was bitter in her mouth, and might-have-beens scorched her heart.

On Wednesday, Henrietta paid her a visit.

"Juliana—you look so pale! Come, ring for tea and we'll have a cozy chat in your salon."

"Not the salon." She said the words too quickly, but the air there was too full of Robert's presence for her to be comfortable. It would be impossible to sit and talk calmly, with the memory of his kisses hot upon her skin.

"Very well," Henrietta said, tilting one eyebrow up.

She handed her hat and gloves to the butler and gave Juliana a keen look. There would be no escaping Hen's questions, and truthfully, Juliana was relieved that there was *someone* she could tell.

"We'll go up to my rooms," Juliana said. "There's no fire in the salon hearth today."

Indeed, they could barely afford coals to heat the bedrooms. She had told the remaining staff how desperate the situation was, but reassured them she was taking steps to remedy the situation. The butler, the housekeeper, and one maid were staying—at least for now. Sadly, the cook had gone to another family. The housekeeper was taking over kitchen duties, with rather dismal results.

Henrietta settled on the window-seat in Juliana's room, then gave her a searching look.

"You've cried off all invitations this past week," she said. "Whatever are you thinking? There's no way you can catch a husband if you spend all your time hiding."

"I…" Juliana trailed her fingers down the slightly dusty curtains. "My circumstances have changed."

"What? How?" Her friend leaned forward and studied her. "You certainly don't look happy about it."

"Father's notes have been bought up. We're safe from debtor's prison." She wet her lips and turned to stare out the window.

"Oh?" Henrietta's eyebrows climbed. "His debts were paid… by whom?"

"Robert Pembroke, Earl of Eastbrook." Juliana clutched the curtains in one hand.

"Heavens! That certainly changes things. Let me think." Henrietta leaned back, pursing her lips. "I presume Robert has paid you a visit?"

Juliana nodded. How could she explain the knots of fear and desire twisting inside her?

"He must still be in love with you!" Henrietta said. "Is that why you've abandoned the pursuit of a husband? Does he have intentions toward you?"

"No. Not… in the way you mean."

Her friend sat up straight, shock widening her eyes. "Never say he's forcing you to be his mistress! What a dreadful—"

"Hen, stop. I am redeeming father's debts, yes. But it is only for five kisses."

"Five kisses? Are you quite certain he no longer cares for you?" Henrietta shook her head. "And five kisses may *seem* harmless, but look at where they could lead."

"I know it." *All too well.* "So far, I have not kissed him—he has kissed me."

She tried to ignore the heat that flashed through her when she thought of his lips on her skin.

"Besides," she added, "I'm certain his only motive is revenge."

Although… there had been that look on his face, after she took her hairpins back. No. She must not torture herself by imagining he still cared for her.

"Juliana. Just because of what happened in the past, doesn't mean—" Henrietta clearly was about to launch into a lecture, when the maid knocked at the door.

"Tea, mistress."

"Come," Juliana called.

She engaged Henrietta in chitchat about the balls she had attended recently as the maid set the tea things out. Finally, the girl finished and left the room.

"Tea?" Juliana moved to the small table and poured out a cup.

Henrietta surveyed the table dubiously.

"Whatever are these?" She poked at a plate of lumpy brown items.

"Scones." Juliana tried to smile. "I know, they look dreadful, but with plenty of jam they are edible. Sadly, the housekeeper is not the best cook."

Henrietta took a sip of tea, then regarded Juliana steadily over the rim of her cup. "Be sensible, Juliana. You may not have creditors turning you out on the streets, but you're certainly not out of financial difficulty. It's imperative you find a wealthy husband."

"I suppose." She dropped a lump of sugar into her cup, and stirred.

The swirl of liquid was like her own thoughts—going round and round, leading nowhere. But Henrietta was right. Staying at home would do no good. Her father was certainly not going to be of any help, either—it was up to her to restore the family's fortunes.

"The Caswell's ball is Friday evening," Henrietta said. "Viscount Wrenforth will be there, and he is your best hope. You must attend. Oh, and do leave off stirring your tea. I'm quite certain the sugar has dissolved, and the noise is making me peevish."

Putting Henrietta in a peevish mood was something to be avoided at all costs. Juliana quickly set her spoon down and took a sip.

"As usual," she said, "nothing but pearls of wisdom fall from your lips."

"Hmph." Henrietta could not quite hide her smile. "A pity we can't string them into a necklace for you to sell. That would nicely solve all your problems."

"A rich husband will have to suffice. Viscount Wrenforth is pleasant enough."

Henrietta nodded. "And his annual income is *much* larger than his nose. It's all a question of comparison."

Indeed, that was part of the problem. Viscount Wrenforth did not compare at all well when measured up against Robert Pembroke. Juliana gave herself a mental shake, and forced herself to take a bit of scone as penance.

"Very well," she said. "I will attend the Caswell's ball on Friday."

The memory of Robert might haunt her past, but she must look to the future.

~CHAPTER FIVE~

The next Thursday, Juliana was again waiting for him in the parlor. She stood at the window, and despite the drab dress she wore, the light silhouetted her pert breasts. Robert smiled. He had plans for those breasts.

He closed the parlor door behind him, then prowled over to where she stood.

"Watching for me, Juliana?" he asked.

"Hardly. I would not still be gazing out the window, were that the case."

She did not turn her head to look at him, which he found amusing. It was a sign of how deeply he was beginning to affect her.

Are you quite certain you are unaffected, in turn? He shook off the ridiculous notion. His heart had finished with Juliana the day she had ground it under her bootheel.

He came up behind her and let his breath feather against the side of her neck. "Your hair is styled as deplorably as ever. Let me take it down for you."

She shot him a glance over her shoulder. "Unless you are planning to kiss my hair, it will remain as it is."

"Tempting… but it's not your hair that I plan to ravish today."

He set his hands at her waist, and felt her tremble, ever so slightly.

"You have kissed my hand," she said, "and my neck—

what is next? My elbow perhaps? My knee?"

He let out a soundless laugh, then drew one finger down her arm. "You were jesting, but the hollow of the elbow is very sensitive. As is the back of the knee."

Her skin was warm and soft in the crook of her elbow. He made a lazy circle there with the tip of his finger, and she drew in a breath.

"Had we more kisses, and time," he said, "I'd begin behind your knee and kiss my way up."

He slid his palm down the side of her thigh, half-expecting her to bolt out from under his caress. But she stayed, her breath quickening. His prior study of seduction was serving him well.

"I'd let my lips explore," he continued, "along the delicate skin of your thigh. Until I reached the most sensitive spot on a woman's body. Do you know where that is, Juliana?"

She shook her head, ever so slightly. The scent of orange-flower water wafted from her hair.

"Here." He moved his hand, letting it brush lightly over the sweet place between her legs.

At that, she gasped and pulled away. She whirled to face him, her cheeks pink with outrage. And arousal.

"You are scandalous! How dare you—"

"Never forget what you owe me," he said. "But don't fear. The secret place between your legs is safe from my kisses. For today."

Her eyes widened. Excellent. He'd planted the seed of an idea that would bedevil her—the anticipation of his final kiss. When he at last kissed her there, at her center, when he made her gasp and writhe and explode with pleasure, then his victory would be complete.

He would be branded on her soul, and she would never be able to escape the memory of him.

"Sit," he said, gesturing to the settee. "It will be more comfortable for both of us."

"Will you hurry and get this blasted kiss over with?" She perched on the cushions and folded her arms. "I've far more important things to attend to this afternoon."

"Mm." He sat next to her. "I have every intention of making you forget those things."

She lifted her chin, and said in a haughty voice, "I doubt that, Lord Eastbrook. But by all means, proceed."

Despite her words, he could see her pulse fluttering wildly. He leaned forward and slowly drew one shoulder of her gown down. She let out a breath and uncrossed her arms, but she said nothing more.

Good. He was done with talking. There were other, better, uses for his mouth now. He continued to pull her gown down, revealing the white fabric of her chemise. Her skin was pale, and smooth as satin. Slowly, he folded her chemise back, revealing the pert slope of her breast.

"Robert," she whispered.

"Shh."

Four springtimes ago, he had longed to caress her this way. He had kissed her breasts through the fabric of her dress, not daring to do more. Now, though, everything between them had changed.

He tugged the cloth down, exposing her entire sweet breast. Her nipple was dusky pink, and beginning to tighten. Oh, but he would make it stand up, a taut bud of desire. Despite the urge to caress her with his fingers, he controlled himself. He wanted her to feel keenly the warmth of his mouth, the wet coaxing of his tongue.

Slipping his hands around to brace her, he dipped his head and took the peak of her breast between his lips. She let out a gasping sigh, and he felt tremors race through her. With his tongue, he lapped at her nipple, encouraging it to stand. Her body did not need much coaxing—in moments she was taut.

He continued to kiss her breast, alternately flicking his tongue against her nipple, then drawing it into the warmth of his mouth. She moaned, and her body betrayed her yet again as she arched her back. He risked a glance at her face. Her eyes were closed, her cheeks flushed, her lovely lips parted. Excellent.

Slowly, he moved one hand down to the place between her legs. She did not seem to notice, except to breathe more deeply. She was warm there, heated from her desire. He gently rubbed the cloth of her dress, sending her arousal higher without shocking her. Like blowing on the embers of a fire, stoking it until it could not help but blaze up. He was patient—and he did not want her to burn up, quite yet.

At last he pulled back. She lay there a moment, eyes still closed, her entire body a sigh. Her nipple was still tantalizingly alert... but no. He was finished, for now. Still, he could not help the vision that flashed through his mind—Juliana lying in his bed, her golden hair spread gloriously about her, her face dreamy with desire.

She opened her eyes. The disarming softness in her expression quickly fled as she sat upright and pulled her gown back into place.

"That makes three," she said, scooting awkwardly away

from him. "I will see you next week, sir."

He stood, oddly sorry for the change in her manner. "Good day, then. And… pleasant dreams."

Her eyes widened, and he let out a low chuckle. There was no doubt his plans were ripening perfectly. Two more kisses, and Juliana Tate would never be the same.

~CHAPTER SIX~

"You dance quite well, Miss Tate." Viscount Wrenforth smiled at her as he guided her off the Caswell's dance floor.

"Thank you, my lord. I've always enjoyed the quadrille."

A pity the viscount was not lighter on his feet—she had narrowly avoided having her toes crushed. It seemed he attributed her quickstepping out of his way to skill and grace, rather than self-preservation.

"Would you…" the viscount cleared his throat. "Would you like to see the conservatory? Lord Caswell was telling me about a new orchid he has acquired."

Juliana studied Viscount Wrenforth from beneath her lashes. Was he hoping to snatch a moment alone, or were his intentions more of a scientific nature?

"Are you botanically inclined, my lord?"

The tip of his large nose turned pink. "No, no. I simply thought ladies enjoyed flowers… but no matter, if you aren't interested—"

"Oh, I am! I would be delighted to view the orchid with you."

This was a very good sign. If she managed the next half-hour correctly, she'd be well on her way to securing a proposal from the viscount. And, truly, there was nothing objectionable about the fellow. Scores of young women would be pleased to trade places with her.

She took the viscount's arm and let him lead her to the side door of the ballroom. Across the way, Henrietta widened her eyes and gave Juliana a significant look. She then caught her aunt's elbow, turning their chaperone away from the sight of Juliana and Viscount Wrenforth departing the ballroom.

It was quieter in the hallway, the length of carpeting muffling their footsteps. Juliana shot a sideways glance at the viscount. Had she misjudged him—was her virtue in any danger? He didn't *seem* the type to whisk a young lady into an unoccupied room and have his way with her, and there was no gossip to suggest he was a scoundrel.

Not like other gentlemen of her acquaintance.

"You're frowning, Miss Tate. Is everything well?"

"Certainly." She pasted a smile on her face. "Do tell me more about Lord Caswell's orchid."

Oh, that was foolish. She should be asking questions about *him*, drawing him out, making him feel as though he was the most pleasant of company. *That* was how one managed a gentleman.

"I don't know much about the orchid," he said. "Only that it is new. And white, apparently. He could talk of nothing else at the Club today, and encouraged everyone to come admire it at the ball. Ah, here we are."

He opened a door decorated with a large cut-glass panel and ushered her inside. Warm, moist air enfolded her, and Juliana sighed. Warmth was becoming a luxury, now that they were being so careful with the coals at home.

If she were a clever girl, all that was about to change.

"Tell me, Lord Wrenforth." She squeezed his arm slightly. "What are your interests? I find myself fascinated to know."

"You do?"

The tip of his nose turned pink again, either with pleased

embarrassment or because of the heat. It was too bad—the viscount needed nothing that drew attention to his overlarge proboscis.

"Yes," she lied. "Do you like horses, perhaps? Or literature?"

She and Robert had lain under the apple trees, reading Shakespeare to one another. With a silent curse, Juliana folded the memory and shoved it into the corner of her mind.

"Actually," the viscount said, "I don't read much. But I am rather fond of dentistry."

Juliana blinked at him. "As in... teeth?"

"Don't worry." He patted her hand, where it lay on his arm. "Yours are quite passable."

"Um." She could not think of an appropriate reply. "Oh, look—that must be the orchid!"

She slipped her arm free from his and quickened her steps toward that glimpse of white, grateful for the distraction. The viscount hurried to keep up with her as she brushed past an array of large ferns. She arrived at a low dais, where the flower in question sat in isolated splendor in a large blue-glazed pot.

It was, without question, the ugliest bloom Juliana had ever seen—protuberant and pallid, at the end of a long bare stalk. The thing almost looked more like a fungus than a flower.

Viscount Wrenforth came up beside her, and they stood for a moment, regarding the orchid.

"It's very... white," he said at last.

"Whiter than teeth," Juliana said, then instantly regretted it. "The petals are so, um..." She could not bring herself to assign an adjective to them.

"Well." He glanced about, then took a step closer. "I'm very pleased you came to view it with me. Although you are lovelier than that orchid."

Considering the flower in question, it was not much of a compliment. Still, she gave him an encouraging smile.

"Thank you, my lord."

It was clear he was thinking of kissing her. Juliana leaned toward him and widened her eyes.

After a tense second, he came even closer and dipped his head. She let out a silent breath of relief, though his large nose grew even larger as it approached her face. Juliana closed her eyes and tilted her face up. Their noses bumped together for an unfortunate moment. Then his lips landed on hers, warm, if a bit unfirm.

He did not enfold her in his arms, or kiss her as though he craved the taste of her. Juliana shifted, trying to give him encouragement, but it did not seem to help. The cold tip of his nose pressed distractingly against her cheek.

"Excuse me." The voice was chilly, and all too familiar. "I hope I'm not interrupting anything important."

Viscount Wrenforth pulled abruptly away. Heart sinking to her toes, Juliana opened her eyes. She was relieved the kiss was ended—but that was the only good thing about the interruption. Slowly, she turned her head.

Robert Pembroke stood, arms folded, on the far side of the hideous orchid. His features were controlled, but temper sparked in his amber eyes.

"Eastbrook," the viscount said, blinking rapidly. "Have you come to see our host's flower?"

"No." Robert did not take his gaze from Juliana. "I will escort Miss Tate back to the ballroom. Good evening, sir."

It was a clear dismissal.

"I, er…" The viscount glanced from Robert to Juliana, then back again. "I see. Good evening, Eastbrook. Miss Tate."

He ducked his head in farewell, then turned and hurried away. She did not know whether to be thankful or dismayed that he had capitulated so easily. The ferns swayed closed behind him, and then she was alone with Robert Pembroke.

"What were you doing with Wrenforth?" Robert asked, circling the orchid. His voice was cold.

"I think it was clear enough." She held her ground. "You are not the only gentleman interested in kissing me. And at least *he* has honorable intentions."

Robert made a sound like a low growl. "Stay out of his company."

"I shall do no such thing! And I would thank you to stay out of my business, and stop scaring off my suitors. Viscount Wrenforth is a perfect gentleman in every way."

Not to mention her only hope for pulling her family from the brink of destitution.

"Perfect gentlemen," Robert said, "do not lure young ladies into conservatories and steal kisses."

"Oh, and I suppose a scoundrel like you would know all about such things."

Her words were meant to be scathing, but came out a bit breathless. Robert was standing uncomfortably close, staring down at her with a possessive expression on his handsome face.

"Indeed," he said. "I *do* know about such things. Allow me to demonstrate."

He took her by the upper arms and, before she had time to gather her wits, drew her against him. His touch was firm, but not so hard that Juliana felt trapped. One quick wrench and she could have been out of his grasp—had she wanted to free herself. Her treacherous heart beat so loudly she expected the nearby foliage to tremble from the force of it.

Then his mouth descended over hers, and she closed her eyes. His tongue traced a wicked line along the seam of her lips. Sparks whirled through her and, despite herself, she let out a little sigh. This, this was the kind of wicked kiss that lured young ladies into conservatories.

His lips coaxed hers open, and his tongue dipped into her mouth. Oh heavens—this was nothing like the lovely, fumbling kisses they had shared four spring-times ago. A taste of the wild and forbidden seared along her senses. This was plundering and surrender, the hot twining of desire whirling between them. She clutched his shoulders, trying to keep the heady sensation from pulling her under.

His hands moved restlessly over her gown, one palm coming up to cup her breast. The peak tingled from his touch, then tightened even more when he swept his thumb across it. With his other arm behind her, he pulled her close. The heat of him seared along her entire body. His thighs were tautly muscled, pressed against hers, and there was an unmistakable bulge between his legs. It gave her an odd thrill, to know that she affected him so.

Then Robert deepened the kiss, his mouth demanding over hers, and she was lost.

There was no ball, no conservatory, no London night spread out darkly behind the glass. Only this—two bodies locked in an embrace, hardness against softness, mouths melding into sweet fire.

Long moments later, he broke the kiss. She blinked up at

him, trying to catch her breath.

"That...that's four," she said, her voice unsteady.

The hint of warmth in his eyes was instantly extinguished. "We had best return you to the ballroom. It wouldn't do for people to gossip about what a lightskirt you've become, Juliana."

Stung, she pulled away. "I can find my way back alone, thank you."

"No." There was no room for argument in his tone. "I wouldn't want you to wander into any more trouble. After you, milady."

He waved at the fern-draped pathway. Squaring her shoulders, Juliana marched forward, far too aware of Robert behind her. Her body still sparked and hummed with the aftermath of their kiss.

This evening had been an utter disaster.

***

Robert scowled as he stalked down the steps of the Caswell's mansion. He couldn't leave that damned ball fast enough. Curse him for giving in to the impulse to attend—though clearly Juliana needed looking after. She was asking to be ruined, going off with Wrenforth like that. Although, admittedly, the viscount was not the ravishing kind.

Still, if anyone was going to ruin Juliana Tate, it would be him. *He* had saved her fortunes, and she owed him dearly for that. Bedamned if he was going to let another man take the prize.

As soon as he returned home, he was going to pen the viscount a letter, warning him well away from Miss Tate. He had no doubt Wrenforth would comply.

How dare that huge-nosed fellow put his hands on Juliana, let alone kiss her? Robert was half-tempted to call him out. But no—that would only add to the titters and raised eyebrows that had met their return to the ballroom. Not that the *ton's* trivial gossip mattered to him. He had only one goal.

Robert balled his hands and strode on, little caring that the wind whipped his coat fiercely behind him. It matched his mood well. A bit of driving sleet would have added the finishing touch. A pity it was May.

Wrenforth had made him waste one of those tremendously expensive kisses. Robert had plans for those five kisses, each one mapped out to ensnare Juliana's senses. But no—his careful seduction had been overturned by the primal instinct to possess.

Revenge was a damned complicated beast.

No matter, he still had one kiss left. Despite the wasted opportunity this evening, he had no doubt of the outcome.

It would only take him one more afternoon to finish cracking Juliana Tate's heart into a dozen pieces.

~CHAPTER SEVEN~

"Juliana!" Henrietta rushed down the hall and gave her a hug, under the disapproving eye of the butler. "Your hat and pelisse are simply soaked. Come to the drawing room, and I'll ring for tea immediately."

"I left in such haste, I forgot my umbrella," Juliana said. "I didn't think coming up the walk would make me so wet."

As if to punctuate her words, rain spattered heavily against the sidelights on either side of Henrietta's mahogany front door. It was one of those spring days filled with sudden squalls—one moment the sun peeking cheerfully out from behind silver-limned clouds, the next, dark and ferocious rain pounding the cobblestones.

In the drawing room, Henrietta pulled two chairs up to the hearth and insisted Juliana take the closest one.

"I'll not have you catching a chill and wasting away like some tragic heroine," her friend said.

Juliana laced her icy fingers together. Although she was nearly sitting in the coals, little heat penetrated the cold that gripped her.

"I'm afraid I'm headed in that direction in any case," she said. "The tragic heroine, I mean. I received a letter today from Viscount Wrenforth."

She swallowed, fear a heavy lump in her chest. But surely Henrietta would know what to do—her friend could always be relied upon for some kind of solution.

"Goodness." Henrietta's eyes widened. "Has he heard

the gossip, then?"

Juliana shivered. "What gossip? And that reminds me—why didn't you tell me the *ton* calls me the Ice Maiden?"

"I knew it would only wound you. Besides, there's no truth to it!"

"Truth has very little bearing on what the scandalmongers say—you know that as well as I." Juliana frowned at her friend. "Now, what current gossip are you referring to?"

"I'm afraid they're saying that you are...er," Henrietta bit her lip, "dallying with the Earl of Eastbrook."

"Dallying? You mean, that I'm his current mistress?" Juliana dropped her gaze to her hands. "I suppose it would appear to be the case—though I've told you Robert holds me in no regard. It is nothing more than a payment of debts owed."

She knew that was true. Why, then, did her foolish soul try to believe otherwise?

The blood was finally returning to her fingers, making them sting fiercely. Now if only her toes would unthaw. And her heart? She only wished it were frozen as solid as the gossips claimed.

"Tell me." Henrietta leaned forward. "What did Viscount Wrenforth say in his letter?"

"Oh, Hen." Juliana blinked back the sharp sting of tears. "He said that I should not misinterpret his attentions, and that while he found me admirable, he would prefer to do so from a greater distance. He wished me well, and farewell—all in four miserly sentences."

"Blast it." Henrietta handed over her handkerchief, then pursed her lips in thought. "Viscount Wrenforth is an unfortunate coward. You are better off without him. Truly, it was a narrow escape. Just think of being wedded to that nose for the rest of your life."

Juliana wiped her eyes. "If only his character were as strong as his nose, he'd be an admirable gentlman. But I'm quite certain he let Robert run him off without a protest."

"Well then, we will simply have to come up with another plan."

"I don't think I can snare a husband, with the gossip circulating that I am Robert's mistress." She wadded Henrietta's kerchief between her hands. "Viscount Wrenforth seems proof enough of that."

Henrietta gave a short nod. "Then there is only one thing you can do. If Robert Pembroke is going to be so careless with your reputation, you must negotiate new terms."

~CHAPTER EIGHT~

It was the last Thursday. The last kiss.

Robert strode into the Tate's town house, anticipation firing his steps. The culmination of his revenge lay within his grasp. He dismissed the emptiness that echoed just behind the thought. Of course he would be slightly adrift, after striving for so long toward this one goal. But the thrill of victory would carry him through.

He entered the parlor, closing the door firmly behind him. Juliana was waiting for him—but instead of standing warily behind the settee, she was sitting upon it. Her hair was loosely bound up in a style that looked vaguely Grecian, and her gown had been altered to a more flattering cut.

"Robert." She inclined her head, light sheening over her golden hair.

What had happened to the stiff, unyielding Juliana? Yes, the kiss in the conservatory had been incendiary, but it hadn't changed anything between them.

Or had it? Did she now fancy herself in love with him? Triumph flashed through him. He had won.

"I…" She wet her lips. "Sit down. Please. We have something to discuss."

He waited a moment, to show he wasn't hers to command, then lowered himself to the settee. The length of his thigh pressed against hers, but she did not shift away.

"I don't intend to waste my time today in talking," he said.

Her cheeks flushed a delicate pink. "I'm well aware that my debt is not yet paid. But, Lord Eastbrook, I must ask. Is your intent to ruin me completely?"

"Ruin you? No, not at all."

He wanted Juliana in pain, brought low—but not in a literal sense. Reducing her to poverty or destroying her social standing had never been his aim. He wanted her to suffer exactly as he had. Nothing more, nothing less.

"Are you quite certain?" She let out a dry laugh. "Your association with me is not going unremarked. Perhaps you require more than five kisses, after all."

"Are you accusing me of breaking my word?" He kept his voice even, though his temper spiked. "I assure you, once I have taken this final kiss, I will be done with you."

"You may be finished with me, but the *ton* will believe you are just beginning." She raised her chin and stared him straight in the eye. "You have frightened off the only suitor I had, and no more will be forthcoming."

"Don't tell me Viscount Wrenforth was truly essaying for your hand?" The thought made something uncomfortably stir inside him.

"Of course he was!" She narrowed her eyes. "Do you think I'm that unworthy? And now... now my family is ruined. He was my only chance to make a match that could have saved us."

"*I* saved you."

"You did not. You only kept us from debtor's prison. All our money is gone, Robert. We have nothing." She dropped her head, despair clear in the curve of her shoulders.

"What about the estate, the rents?" An odd, hollow feeling beat through him. Had he misjudged so badly?

Juliana's family had never been tremendously well off, but their property had brought in a tidy annual sum. Not much, compared to what Robert now held as the Earl of Eastbrook, but certainly enough to keep the Tate family in comfort.

"Father mortgaged everything." Her voice was nearly a whisper. "We have until the end of the month, and then even this townhouse will be gone."

Damn it. He should have investigated more closely when he'd bought up her father's debts. His gaze went to her hands, clasped so tightly in her lap that her knuckles were white.

This was not the victory over Juliana he had planned. He was suddenly chilled, unsure of his direction.

"Take me, Robert." She raised desperate eyes to him. "I'm ruined in the eyes of the *ton*—you heard the gossip at the Caswell's ball, as well as I. Now that Wrenforth has flown, no one will believe…" She swallowed. "Make me your mistress."

"No!" The word was out before he could even consider it.

Juliana as his mistress—somehow he could not stomach the notion, despite his carefully planned seduction. He could not use her in such a fashion, no matter what she had done to him. Though he could scarcely admit it, she deserved better than a life forever tainted by scandal.

Her face went pale and he caught the sparkle of tears in her eyes before she turned her head away.

Bloody hell. How had it gone so wrong? He was at an utter loss.

"This was not what I had intended." He grated the words out. "Consider your debt paid. I will have your father's notes delivered to you later today."

He rose, and she looked up sharply, misery still etched on her face.

"You can't simply leave," she said.

There was nothing else he *could* do. Surely some solution would come to him—but not now, while his thoughts were so impossibly tangled with the sight of her.

He could not even bid her farewell. Victory turned to ashes in his mouth as he strode out of the parlor. He collected his hat and gloves from the butler, then stormed out onto the walk.

He was brought up short by the sight of an umbrella pointed directly at his midriff.

"Halt right there, Robert Pembroke," a shrill voice said.

A young lady dressed in violet stood before him. She looked vaguely familiar… ah yes, the Brightstone girl, Juliana's bosom friend. Possibly the only person in London who knew of their previous acquaintance.

"Miss Brightstone." He tipped his hat, then tried to move past.

"You, sir, will remain here until I've said my piece." She brandished her umbrella at him.

Robert took a careful step back. "I pray it's short—I'm required elsewhere. Miss Tate would doubtless be glad of your company. She's a bit overset."

"Whatever you have done to Juliana," the young lady said, "she is blameless."

"I think not." He bit the words out.

"You're being a complete fool." She glared at him. "Why would Juliana scheme to break your heart? She was terribly in love with you. I dare say, she still is."

"Her parting words to me four years ago indicated

otherwise."

"You don't think her dragon of a mother had anything to do with that?" Miss Brightsone stamped her foot.

"Even if she did, Juliana could have shown some spine! We were planning..." He checked himself. How much did Miss Brightstone know?

"To run away together, yes. And Juliana would have, too, except that her mother caught wind of it. But do you know who bore the brunt?"

Robert shook his head. So far, there was nothing in Miss Brightstone's tale to make him change his mind about Juliana's faithlessness.

"Her brother." The young lady lowered her umbrella. "Her younger brother, who was locked in his wardrobe—his wardrobe!—without any food, until Juliana broke it off with you. Their mother would have starved him for days. The sound of his crying was horrible." She met his gaze. "Do you really think Juliana should have abandoned her brother in order to run off with you?"

"I... didn't know. Blast it! She could have told me."

His memory of the past was suddenly tilted—all the things he had thought true now cast in an odd, sideways light. Had Juliana loved him, after all? Had his revenge been built on a lie? The cold suspicion of it crept through his bones.

"She could not have told you—not and kept her brother safe. You had to believe completely that she was done with you, or her brother would pay the consequences, over and over. Their mother..." Miss Brightstone looked away. "She was not a pleasant woman."

His heart gave a bitter lurch. "Juliana was quite convincing."

"She had to be. Oh, try to understand what it was like for her! Her heart broke as much as yours did. Maybe even more."

Robert shook his head, attempting to settle his thoughts into some semblance of order. Only one thing was clear—he must see Juliana again, immediately. He spun on his heel and headed back toward the front door.

"Wait!" Miss Brightstone cried.

He ignored her, ignored the butler's startled expression as he strode past, and flung open the parlor door.

Juliana looked up. Her eyes widened—clearly she had been weeping.

"Robert!" She scrambled to her feet, a handkerchief clutched in one hand. "What are you—"

"Why didn't you tell me?" He took her by the shoulders and searched her expression. "Juliana—if I had known you still cared for me four years ago, I would have crossed fire to be with you. I would have slain dragons."

She swallowed. "My mother… was a dragon in truth. But how did you find out?"

"I met Miss Brightstone coming up the walk." A shiver moved through him. Had the young lady been a minute later, he never would have known the truth. Juliana would be lost to him. Forever, this time. "You should have told me."

She bit her lip. "Secrecy is… a difficult habit to break. We had to keep silence on so many things, my brother and I. There was nothing you could have done, Robert."

His heart twisted inside him. They had *both* suffered, and he had thought to punish her for it? After what she'd had to endure, he felt like a blind fool.

"I should have realized," he said. "I would have taken

you away from there in a heartbeat."

"And my brother, too? Supported us, hidden us?" She shook her head. "I know you would have tried—but I could not have asked it of you."

He wanted to argue with her, wanted to unwind the past and make different, better choices—but perhaps she was right. He let out a breath. They had been so young, full of innocence about the world. Faced with such difficulty, he wanted to think they could have triumphed—but he would never know.

"Then why didn't you tell me, once your mother was dead?"

"You hated me." She turned her face away. "And I could not blame you for it. Besides, you wouldn't have believed me."

"I believe you now."

He did. The past had righted itself, and now shone with a bright clarity. What was done could not be undone, and he would always be sorry for it—but the future lay, full of sudden promise, before them.

"Juliana—forgive me. I…" He cleared his throat. "I needed a reason to see you, to kiss you—and told myself it was all for revenge."

"I had hoped it was more, though I knew I was yearning for the moon. But I still could not refuse you." She took a deep breath and looked into his eyes, her expression clear and open. "Robert—I love you. I have always loved you."

Damn, she was so courageous it put him to shame.

"I love you, Juliana."

His voice was low, rough against the word he had sworn did not exist. The word his heart had newly discovered, buried as it had been under years of lies.

Love.

What an idiot he had been, twisting his own feelings into a mockery of the truth. A buried fragment of the Shakespeare they had used to quote floated up in his mind.

"*Eternity was in our lips and eyes*," he said, touching her cheek.

"Antony and Cleopatra." She smiled up at him. "Oh, but we will not come to such a bitter end after all, will we?"

"It's been bitter enough—for both of us. I'm so terribly sorry, my love." He wanted to sweep her into his arms and kiss her senseless. "The day you turned me away, I was coming to ask you…"

For a moment that young man lay just beneath his skin, striding up the blossom-filled lane, a simple gold ring in his pocket and a heart full of nothing but light.

"I know." She sounded breathless.

He slipped the heavy signet ring of the Earls of Eastbrook from his finger.

"Bedamned if I'm going to waste another moment—or risk losing you again." He went down on one knee on the threadbare carpet and took her hand. "Juliana Charlotte Tate, will you do me the very great honor of becoming my wife?"

"I…" Her eyes were bright, and a smile trembled on her lips. "Oh Robert—I will!"

He slid the ring onto her finger and closed her hand over it, then rose and gathered her tightly to him. The scent of orange-flower water was suddenly the happiest smell in the entire world. He dipped his head and inhaled deeply, letting the golden crown of her hair tickle his face.

"There is one thing," she said, her voice muffled against

his coat.

"Yes?" He loosened his embrace so that he could look directly at her.

"The matter of a final kiss." Her cheeks flushed a becoming pink. "That is, I believe there is one more payment owed. In a certain… place."

He nearly laughed out loud. So she *had* been thinking of his mouth there, between her legs. Ah, but he was going to seduce her, again and again, for years to come.

"I see you are going to be a delightfully wanton wife."

"Since I have no dowry, I'm afraid I must owe you kisses for that as well." She gave him a look edged with mischief. "How many, do you think? Five hundred?"

"Five thousand, at least. And I owe you that many in turn, in penance."

"I would think you do." She was laughing at him, now. "Be careful, my lord. I may lead you into conservatories and kiss you most wickedly."

"Good—I expect nothing less."

"Ten thousand kisses…" She laced her fingers behind his neck and pulled his head down toward hers. "I think we'd best begin right away."

Their lips touched, and for a moment he smelled apple blossoms. Something in his soul stilled, the bitterness of four years dissolving in a rain of white petals.

He would never grow weary of the taste of her. His Juliana—at last.

~THE END~

Anthea Lawson

Maid for Scandal

It was a splendid idea—or had seemed so at the time. Impersonate a maid in order to be close to Giles Wildering for two glorious weeks. How daring!

Anna Harcourt frowned at the pail of soapy water in front of her and resisted the urge to fling her scrub-brush down the hall. The very long hall, patterned in black and white marble, and exceedingly uncomfortable on her knees. The hall which she was now responsible for scrubbing to a flawless shine.

When she first conceived of the disguise, it had seemed perfect. The family of her best friend, Belinda Caswell, owned a nearby estate. She would pretend to be staying with the Caswells, while secretly masquerading as a maid at the Wildering's mansion. Belinda was delighted to help Anna with her deception.

"It's like something from a novel!" Belinda had said as they laid their plans.

Besides, it was the only way Anna could see Giles—he of the bright blue eyes and flattering words. Just think, to breathe the same air, to see him on a daily basis and let the fresh bud of their new love come to full flower. She had no doubt she would end the summer transformed, no longer inexperienced Anna Harcourt, but a true lady, known by the name of Mrs. Giles Wildering.

She had thought that, as soon as she arrived, Giles would somehow feel it in the air. He would come and sweep her off her feet, and…. Well, in truth, her imagination had not carried her much beyond arriving at Wildering Hall.

Unfortunately, there were a number of practicalities she had failed to take into account. First, she'd no idea how much the utter drudgery of servant's work would keep her away from the house's grander inhabitants. Secondly, as the most junior member of the staff, she was allotted the worst of tasks. And thirdly, perhaps most horribly, she had to rise at an excruciating hour, when the light of dawn was only a pale thought in the sky.

No one to gently open her curtains after nine-o-clock, or bring her a pot of hot chocolate. No one to stir up her coals and make sure her dressing-gown was laid out. Instead, a bowl of porridge and a scrub-brush had ushered her into her first day as a maid.

"Stop your daydreaming, and get to work!" Mrs. Foutch, the housekeeper, marched to where Anna knelt. "The family will wake in one hour, and this hallway had better be spotless. Spotless and *dry*."

"Yes, ma'am." Anna mumbled the words, trying not to sound like a governess-educated London miss.

"Lady Caswell recommended you—though I don't know what her ladyship was thinking." The housekeeper sniffed, as if the gentry were wholly inscrutable. "Well then. When you've finished, I'll be in the blue parlor."

Without waiting for a reply, Mrs. Foutch turned away, the clack of her boot-heels quite reproachful. Anna sighed and dipped her brush into the water. The housekeeper was right to be doubtful of her letter of recommendation. Belinda was excellent at forging her mother's hand, but neither of them had known quite what to say. Perhaps they had been too effusive about Anna's supposed qualities as a maid.

As she scrubbed, Anna could not help thinking of Giles. Unfortunately, she had not been able to catch sight of him yesterday when she'd arrived. Later, she'd learned that he had been out riding for most of the afternoon, then off to a gathering of friends. Today, however, he would see her, and all this trouble would be worth it. Anna felt her heart take wing at the thought.

He would recognize her immediately, of course. After all, had they not met secretly on two occasions? Sadly, both times had been too short for more than whispered promises. But at a garden party only a fortnight ago he had held her hand beneath the rose arbor and told her he found her irresistibly beautiful. She had let him steal a kiss—just a small one—but the memory had engraved itself upon her heart.

Then Giles had departed London rather abruptly, leaving only a note imploring her to keep him in her thoughts. Once he had gone, there was no color, no vividness left in her life. She simply couldn't bear it. Her heart was breaking for want of him.

Coming here in disguise was altogether impetuous of her, she knew it—but love admitted no boundaries. Hadn't Shakespeare himself said that very thing? So here she was, and soon she and Giles would be together.

This happy thought carried her to the end of the hall, despite the ache in her arms and the bruises surely forming on her knees. Anna let out a sigh and stood to survey the floor stretching behind her. Why, she had done rather a fine job of it. Perhaps she would make an excellent maid, after all.

Although, as soon as she could speak with Giles, everything would change.

Sadly, the 'young master,' as the butler called him, was a late riser. A very late riser. Anna had completed more chores than she could count and had yet to catch sight of him. The servant's midday meal came, and Cook pressed bread and cheese into Anna's hands, urging her to go out into the sunshine.

"Ye've a bit of a wan face now, dearie. The fresh air will do ye good. Go on then."

Anna gave her a grateful nod, then slipped out the kitchen door before anyone else could speak to her. Except for a red-haired girl who kept staring daggers at her, the other maids and footmen seemed pleasant enough—but Anna couldn't risk becoming friendly. Her pretense was too flimsy, and truly, she had no idea what to say to them.

The kitchen garden was full of rows of lettuces, and the air smelled of thyme and lavender. Anna took a deep breath. Heavens, she was tired. Even wearier than the time she and Belinda had watched the sun come up after dancing all night at the Caswell's annual ball.

A sunlit patch of uncut grass beyond the gate beckoned to her, and she slipped the latch and went to sit in the tall green stems. The bread and cheese were delicious—quite as good as any canapés she had tasted in Town. A pity her lunch was gone so quickly, as it had only taken the edge off her hunger. She let out a deep breath and lay back in the grass, arms pillowed under her head. Just a short rest…

A tremendous crunching sound woke her. Anna opened her eyes, then let out a shriek and scrambled back, away from the long muzzle with enormous teeth chomping the grasses beside her head.

The horse—for indeed, it was—gave a sharp whinny and bobbed its head.

"Here now," a deep male voice said. "What have you found, Windsor? A new kind of squawking bird, come to roost at Wildering Hall?"

A tall, sandy-haired man rounded the horse. When he saw Anna sprawled in the grass, his eyebrows went up, and his green eyes lit with amusement.

She hastily scrambled to her feet, then met his gaze directly. "I'd thank you to control your horse, sir."

They both glanced at Windsor. Although he was an imposing creature—very large and black—he was browsing placidly. She felt her cheeks warm. Clearly she had been in no danger. It was just the abruptness of her waking that had set her nerves on edge.

"Indeed." The man shook his head. His solemn expression was spoiled by the smile that teased the corners of his mouth. "He's a terrible menace. My apologies, miss."

"No matter—I'd best get back to my duties."

Should she drop him a curtsy? The stranger was not particularly finely dressed. Certainly not in such a fashionable state as Giles Wildering—and his rugged features did not compare in the least to the master of the house. The man's cravat was hardly tied, and his coat was worn at the cuffs. Not gentry.

So, then, would a maid curtsy to a groom? Anna smoothed her hands down her cotton skirts. Drat, there was so much she did not know about her supposed station in life.

The man tilted one eyebrow up, and she dropped her gaze, realizing she had been staring at him longer than was proper.

"Don't let me keep you," he said.

"Of course not. Good day, sir." She settled for a quick bob up and down, then hastily made for the kitchen door. Heavens, could that have been any more awkward?

All thoughts of her meeting with the stranger were soon buried beneath a mountain of household chores. After she had dusted the shelves in the library and helped one of the other maids fold the linens, Mrs. Foutch set her to polishing the silver in the butler's pantry.

At least it was easy on the knees, though her fingers were soon smudged with tarnish. Still, she was quite put out. How would Giles ever find her here, tucked away in the pantry?

Then, blessing of blessings, she heard his voice. Anna hastily set down the spoon she was polishing and pulled the door a bit wider. There he was—walking down the hall with the head groom. Giles looked quite splendid, dressed for riding in a dark blue coat that showed his broad shoulders to advantage, with a sky-blue waistcoat beneath. His cravat was tied in a perfect knot, and his boots shone as if they had never been marred by contact with a stirrup.

A little sigh escaped her lips.

He was deep in conversation—she caught something about a new horse as the men approached. Her heart pounded wildly. Any moment now he would lift his head and see her. Anticipation and joy sizzled through her whole body. She opened the door another few inches. Soon, soon.

Now.

Now, their eyes would meet, and his lips would form her name. Anna held her breath. He was a mere yard away…a foot away… close enough for her to reach out and touch his arm...

He walked past. Without even noticing her. Despair washed over Anna, and her breath left her in a low, quiet sob. She nearly called his name aloud in desperation—but it was too late.

Blinking back hot tears, she watched as the two men turned the corner and were gone. Giles had not seen her. He had not for an instant looked up, despite the intensity of her gaze upon him.

She retreated back into the pantry and dabbed at her eyes with the hem of her apron. Giles was mad for horses, she knew it from their second conversation. Clearly his mind had been elsewhere just now. Why, he likely wouldn't have noticed *anyone*, he'd been so engrossed in speaking with the groom.

It was good for a person to have a variety of interests. Indeed, Anna herself was quite fond of riding. Once she and Giles were married, they would have a lovely time discussing horses, she was certain of it. Perhaps they would select a matched pair to ride. Grays. Or no, chestnuts, with lovely dark manes and tails. How handsome they would look together...

"I believe that spoon is quite polished enough." Mrs. Foutch's voice broke into her thoughts. "Finish up here, and then you're needed to help serve tea. Speak with Cook, directly."

"Yes, ma'am," she said, but the housekeeper was already bustling away.

Anna took a few moments to tidy up in the servant's area of the kitchen. She washed her hands, tucked a stray brown curl back under her cap, then presented herself to Cook.

"Have ye a steady hand?" The woman held out a tray piled high with delicacies.

"I do," Anna said, trying not to eye the sandwiches and cakes. Her stomach gave an unfortunate growl.

"Follow Martha here up to the mistress's rooms," Cook said, nodding to the red-haired maid, who was standing beside her. "And take care on the stairs."

Anna lifted the tray and gave Martha a bright smile. "Shall we?"

The other girl scowled, then took up a second tray holding the teapot and cups and turned her back on Anna. Unfriendly indeed—but it was just as well. They had no hope of ever becoming friends, after all. What a shock Martha would have when Anna's engagement to Giles was announced. The servant would become the mistress, much to everyone's surprise. She felt a secret smile cross her face at the thought.

The servant's stairs were narrow and steep, and Anna heeded Cook's advice. She was glad not to be carrying up the teapot. It wouldn't do to arrive in Mrs. Wildering's parlor with a puddle of tea sloshing about on the tray. Although, truth be told, she'd rather not arrive in Mrs. Wildering's parlor at all.

Anna had been introduced to Giles's mother once, although it had been last Season. Still, if Mrs. Wildering recognized her, this charade would be up entirely. Fear beat through her, and her forehead felt clammy.

"Hurry it up!" Martha called. "If the tea's cold, it's your fault." She stood at the narrow door to the second floor, holding it open with one hip.

While Anna was still several feet away, the other maid stepped out into the hall and let the door swing closed. Clutching her tray, Anna ran up the last few steps in order to keep it from shutting in her face.

The carpet was thick under her feet as she followed Martha down the hall to Mrs. Wildering's suite. Anna lagged behind until Martha scowled and tipped her head impatiently at the door. With a deep breath, she followed the other maid inside, trying to keep Martha as a shield between herself and the women seated in the small parlor.

Luckily, Mrs. Wildering paid them no notice as the tea was brought in. She was entertaining visitors—another older woman, and a mousey-looking young lady whom Anna guessed to be about her own age. Thank goodness the guests were strangers to her. The ladies conversed, ignoring the maids as they set their trays down and readied the tea.

"Of course," the visiting matron said in a confiding tone, "you cannot discount my own Eugenia here. She is possessed of many excellent virtues."

The young lady bit her lip and stared down at the floor, as though she wished she could disappear through it. She did not have the advantage of a maid's cap, which Anna had tugged down so it nearly covered her eyes.

"Hm." Mrs. Wildering tapped her cheek with one finger. "The Earl of Blakely's niece is also invited. By all accounts, she is a lovely girl."

"But hardly the same as a viscount's *daughter*." The guest sniffed, while her unfortunate daughter remained silent.

"Would you care for a cup of tea?" Mrs. Wildering turned, and there was Martha, presenting the teapot as though she had known the very moment the mistress would be asking for it.

Anna made sure the plates of delicacies were in no danger of tipping, then slid the tray onto the low table in front of the ladies. None of them even glanced her way.

Heavens, was she so oblivious to her own staff? Although she was grateful to be invisible, it was rather unsettling. She hovered behind the chairs for a moment. Should she stay? Was her presence needed beyond the simple act of carrying up a tray of food, or by leaving would she draw undue attention to herself? She wanted more than anything to be gone from the room.

Martha finished setting out three cups and saucers for Mrs. Wildering, then caught Anna's eye. She nodded to the doorway, and silently the two of them left the mistress's suite. Anna quietly shut the parlor door and turned—only to collide with a gentleman striding down the hall.

"Oh!" she exclaimed.

She looked up, past the finely-embroidered waistcoat and perfectly knotted cravat, to meet a pair of bright blue eyes. Giddy joy galloped through her.

At last. Face-to-face with Giles Wildering. Surely that spark in his eyes was pleased recognition. Anna gazed into his face, and felt as though she could stand there all afternoon, simply looking at him.

"Beg pardon, sir," Martha said, taking her by the elbow and yanking her back.

Ah, yes—the servants always stayed to the edges of the halls. She had forgotten.

"Well, well," Giles said, a smile spreading across his handsome features. "And who have we here?"

"The new maid," Martha said. Her expression was sour. "Do excuse us, sir."

"Wait." He took Anna by the arm. "And what is your name, new maid?"

Didn't he know? Confusion fluttered in her chest for a

moment, until the answer came clear. Of course he recognized her—but thought she might be here under an assumed name. How clever of him not to blurt it out.

"Anna, sir." She gave him a complicit smile, and the expression in his eyes deepened.

"Excellent." He moved his thumb up and down her arm—a small caress. A signal that he understood her deception, and her reasons for it.

Martha made a small humming noise. "Really, sir, we must be going."

"Certainly. Carry on." He let go of Anna's arm, but the warmth of his smile was like a hundred candles burning inside her.

As Martha hauled her down the hall, Anna couldn't help glancing back over her shoulder. Giles was watching her. The look on his face made her shiver with delight.

Oh, she had been so right to come here. The reward was worth every difficulty.

***

The next morning, Martha shook Anna awake before dawn. "Up with you—time to work," she said, her tallow candle casting eerie shadows on the attic walls.

Anna tried not to groan aloud. Her arms and shoulders ached, and all she wanted to do was roll back over and bury her head in her pillow. Only the thought of Giles gave her the will to rise.

After a hurried breakfast of old bread and porridge, Anna was set to work cleaning the grates and hearths. It was sooty, hard work—and best if one breathed shallowly. She had finished with the blue parlor and was nearly done in the drawing room when Martha found her.

"Come," the other maid said, sounding most displeased. "You've a new duty."

Anna wiped her hands on her apron and stood. "What is it?"

Martha gave no answer, only turned and led the way down the opulently decorated hall to the servant's door, cleverly disguised to look like just another mahogany panel. One wouldn't want the maids' comings and goings to be noticeable now, would one? Anna shook her head.

They exited the narrow stairwell on the third floor of the mansion, where the family's bedrooms were, and Martha stalked down the hall until she reached a large door.

"Here," she said.

"Here, what?"

The other maid scowled. "Master Giles's bedchamber. You're to go in and stir up the fire, make the chamber ready. But take care not to wake him."

"*I'm* to do that?" Anna lifted one hand to her chest and felt the eager thumping of her heart.

Giles was so clever, arranging it so that they could meet privately. No doubt he was only feigning sleep, waiting for her to arrive.

"And don't take too long about it, either." Martha's lips pressed together in a most unbecoming manner. "I ought to be the one going in there, mind you."

"Why aren't you?" But she knew the answer.

"Because," the other maid spit out, "he asked for *you*."

With that, Martha turned on her heel and stormed off. Really, such a sour disposition would not serve the girl well.

She ought to take some honey with her daily meals. Although… were servants permitted honey? Thus far, Anna had only been given treacle to sweeten her morning porridge.

But enough thinking about the disagreeable Martha. She had far more important matters to attend to. Giles had asked for her. The knowledge spread warmly through her entire body. Smiling, Anna opened the door.

It was dim in his bedroom. The heavy drapes shut out the mid-morning sun, though there was enough light to see the large bed in the center of the room. A figure lay there, sprawled in sleep. Truly, was he still asleep? She crept closer, until she could make out his features. Dear, handsome Giles. His eyes were closed, his dark hair tousled. Beneath the bedlinens, his chest rose in the deep and regular breath of dreaming.

She swallowed her disappointment. Should she wake him? Yet Martha had cautioned her against that very thing. How vexing. She stood a moment, glancing about the room. The air was a bit cool, and held a faint musky odor. She had never realized how a few coals took the edge of the night's chill from a room. Very well—she would begin by poking up the fire. Loudly.

He stirred, and joy jolted through her. He was waking!

"Are you there?" Giles's voice was blurry with sleep.

"Yes. Yes, I am." She laid the poker down and hurried to the end of the bed.

He blinked at her, then smiled, slow and lazy. "Anna the maid. You are a pretty one."

He had called her beautiful before—but pretty was satisfactory. More than satisfactory, truly. And did it matter the exact words? It was enough that he found her appearance pleasing.

"Thank you, sir." She could not bring herself to call him Giles. It suddenly seemed too forward.

As was being in his bedroom, alone—but that was the price she would pay for love.

"Open the curtains," he said, "then come closer, so I may see you properly."

Anna hurried to pull the drapes wide, and warm light spilled into the room. She turned, catching her breath once again at how perfect Giles's features were, how blue his eyes. He caught her gaze, and beckoned.

"So, Anna. I expect you to take your new duties seriously," he said.

She gave him a tentative smile. Clearly he was amused by her disguise as a maid. She supposed she could indulge him.

"What would those duties be?" she asked.

He propped himself on his elbows. The sheet slid down to reveal his naked chest, and she felt heat flame into her cheeks.

"For a man like myself, a proper beginning to the day might begin with... a kiss."

She placed a hand over her mouth. How reckless he was! "Why sir—that strikes me as most *im*proper."

"All the better." His eyes held a wicked spark. "Come here, Anna, and let me steal a kiss."

Her pulse was beating madly. Slowly, she moved to stand beside him at the edge of the bed. He sat up, paying no heed to his state of undress, and took her by the shoulders. Then, between one breath and the next, his lips were upon hers. Heat flashed through her, and a heady rush of satisfaction. Giles was kissing her.

This kiss, however, was quite different from the one they had shared beneath the rose arbor. He pulled her against him, and her hands came to rest on his naked shoulders. How delicious, how forbidden, his warm skin felt beneath her palms.

But even more scandalous was the movement of his tongue, sweeping insistently across her mouth. She pursed her lips and pressed them more fervently against his.

With a bark of laughter, he broke the kiss. "I see you have much to learn—and I'll gladly teach you." His gaze moved to the ornate clock on the mantel and he frowned. "I fear it's too late, today, however. My valet will be arriving shortly. You'd best be on your way."

She had disappointed him. Regret rushed through her as she stepped away from the bed and straightened her cap.

"I'm sorry." She could not quite conceal the tremble in her voice.

"Don't fret, maid Anna. Simply come earlier tomorrow, and open the curtains as soon as you arrive. Then I'll show you how to rouse me most satisfactorily."

Happiness pushed the last of the worry from her mind. He was not truly sending her away—he cared for her still. "Of course I shall! It will be my pleasure."

"No, my dear." He gave her a rakish smile. "It will be mine."

***

The rest of the morning passed in a rosy haze. Anna scrubbed and swept without complaint, for Giles had kissed her. Although... clearly there had been something unsatisfactory about it, at least to him. She hated to have disappointed him so. What had she done wrong?

The question grew, blazing, until it was a fire scorching her. What had she done wrong? What?

It was a welcome distraction when Cook sent her out to the dairy for more cheese. As she circled the building, something in the woods beyond caught her eye.

A large, dark shape was moving through the trees. Fear flashed through her, but before it could settle under her skin, she realized she was seeing a horse. Without a rider—which likely meant it had gotten loose.

Last summer, her mare, Isolde, had escaped, and she had suffered hours of stomach-knotting worry before her mount had finally been found. Perhaps she could catch this wayward horse, and save someone else that same pain. Anna moved closer to the trees, careful to keep her movements deliberate.

Why, it was Windsor—the horse she had met yesterday. His black bulk was unmistakable. He snorted when he saw her, and stepped back a pace, but at least he didn't bolt. A lead rope dragged on the ground, attached to his halter, but he wore no saddle. Thank goodness he hadn't thrown his rider and gone galloping off.

"Well now, Windsor," she said in a soft voice. "What are you doing out here alone? I'm quite certain they're looking for you."

Watching her with wary brown eyes, Windsor sidled away. She stepped forward again, still speaking quiet nonsense. The horse shivered this time, but stood still.

Drat—if only she had an apple in her pocket to offer. Instead, she bent and pulled up a handful of long-stemmed grasses. Nothing the horse couldn't get for himself, but some creatures liked the attention of being offered food, nearly as well as the treat itself.

Luckily for her, Windsor was a curious one. His soft black ears pricked forward, and he took a hesitant step forward. Anna stood still and held her palm out flat, offering the grasses for his inspection. Just a little closer... then she felt the tickle of horse-lips and a gust of warm air as Windsor whiffled up the grass.

It was a simple thing to give his nose a pat, then catch the lead rope. "Good lad. Let's go find the stables now, shall we?"

He blew out a breath, as if he disagreed. Still, he let Anna lead him out of the trees. She held the rope firmly, in case he changed his mind, and glanced about until she sighted the stables. There seemed to be a great deal of hubbub there—people gesturing and running about. As she approached, leading her new friend, the stable-hands caught sight of her and began calling out urgently. A figure emerged from the shadowed building and strode toward her. He looked vaguely familiar...

Ah, it was the groom she had met yesterday. When he reached her, she found that his eyes were the same startling shade of green she had remembered.

"Have you lost something?" she asked. "I found this fellow wandering about in the woods."

He gave her a curious look. "Why were you in the woods, little bird?"

"I was on my way to the dairy, if you must know. And my name is Anna." It was forward of her, but she truly didn't think the rules of proper introduction were as important among the lower classes. Were they?

"Thank you for retrieving Windsor," he said, holding out

his hand for the rope. "The boys who let him slip away were in a panic—but I think our lad here was just trying to go home."

"Home?" She let him take the horse from her. "Doesn't he belong here?"

"He does now." The man didn't look quite pleased at the fact.

"Oh, is he is Gile—er— Mr. Wildering's new horse?"

"He is." He called one of the stable-boys over and handed him the lead. "Take better care of him, this time."

"We're right sorry, Sir Jonathan. It won't happen again." The boy led the black horse away.

"Now then, Anna." The man set his hands on his hips. "I'll see you back to the house."

"But I—"

"I insist. Besides, I owe you a favor for returning Windsor." He fell into step beside her.

Anna glanced up him. Although he was not truly handsome, there was something quite masculine about him. He looked like—well, like the kind of man who would know the answer to the question that had been burning in her thoughts all day.

A curious sense of freedom winged through her. This man knew nothing of her or her station in life. She was free to ask him anything. And he had said he owed her a favor.

"Mr., er..." All she knew was his given name. She rubbed the hem of her apron between her fingers.

"Simply Jonathan, if you please." His eyes were very green, looking into hers. "Yes?"

The words tumbled out in a rush, before she could consider them too carefully. "Do you know a great deal about kissing?"

His eyebrows rose. "Is that the favor you'd like? A kiss?"

"Oh, no! I didn't mean that at all." She dropped her gaze and fiercely studied the pathway beneath her feet. "An explanation would be quite sufficient."

"Ah." There was a wealth of amusement in his voice. "An explanation. Of kissing."

"Yes." Heat blazed in her cheeks, but she must know. She simply could not disappoint Giles again. "I would like to understand some of the particulars, you see."

"Why don't you tell me what your experience is? I don't want to shock you."

She glanced up. "Can kisses truly be shocking?"

"Indeed." Wicked knowledge gleamed in his eyes. "But we digress. What kind of kissing would you like to know about, Anna?"

"The usual kind?" Goodness, she couldn't conceive what else he might be referring to. "You know. Where a gentleman—er, man—presses his mouth to a woman's."

She couldn't help it—her gaze fell to his lips. They looked surprisingly soft in contrast to his hewn features.

He nodded. "Yes. Go on."

"Go on? I mean... what more is there, beyond the lips coming together?" She twisted the corner of her apron around her fingers.

This, then, was what had disappointed Giles so—the something more. Whatever it might be. Oh, she did so want to please him! And she was protected by her disguise. As far as Jonathan knew, she was a simple country maid asking... well, asking a terribly awkward question, but there was no going back now.

One of Jonathan's eyebrows crept up, though his voice did not reveal any surprise. "I see the nature of your problem."

"You do? Oh, but that is marvelous." She had been right to ask him, no matter how forward it made her seem. Maids were forward, weren't they? "Please tell me—what happens next?"

"Well. When the lips meet, that is often merely the beginning of the kiss. It deepens." He gave her a level look. "The parties involved open their mouths. And touch tongues."

She halted and stared up at him. "What? That sounds dreadful."

"It's not dreadful," he said. "Quite the opposite."

She shook her head. Was this what Giles had been trying to do with her? It was unfathomable.

"Well," she said, uncomfortably aware of the primness of her tone. "Thank you very much. For explaining."

He threw back his head and laughed, a full-throated sound. "An explanation doesn't do it justice. Would you care for a demonstration, so that you may fully understand?"

"I…"

Part of her was urging her to say no, to hurry down the path and leave Jonathan behind. But another part was clamoring yes, yes. This might be her best chance to learn, to please Giles. And who would ever know?

Besides, she did not think Jonathan was the kind to take undue advantage. There was something almost gentlemanly in his bearing, despite his lowly position in the stables. They were almost at the dairy. If he pressed her too much, she could simply scream for help.

A kiss—so that she might know exactly what to do. His reckless suggestion took fire in her blood. She mustered her courage.

"Perhaps…." Her heart sped. "Perhaps you might show me, after all."

He studied her a long moment, and her resolve began to fade. Was her lack of knowledge so off-putting?

"If you have changed your mind, I understand." She turned her head away, so that she would not see pity in his expression. "I suppose I am not the kissable kind."

He lifted his hand and gently turned her face toward him. The feel of his fingers against her cheek made a thrill course all the way down to her feet. There was no pity in his eyes.

"You are eminently kissable, Anna. I confess, I'm surprised you're not an expert on the subject."

Hope fluttered in her chest. "Then you will? Kiss me?"

"Come." He drew her into the shade of the dairy wall, where they would be out of sight of anyone passing by.

They stood facing one another, and then he placed his hands at her waist and pulled her forward. He was taller than Giles, his chest broader. For a moment she kept her hands at her sides, unsure. She stared up at him, certain her eyes were full of questions. Oh dear. Perhaps she shouldn't have…

He lowered his face, his lips gently brushing hers, and her worries fled. The kiss began slowly, simply, yet there was nothing simple in the wild beating of her heart. His lips moved against hers, lightly teasing. She had never known how very sensitive her lips could be—tingling and impatient for more.

Then he settled his mouth more firmly over hers and it felt like the sun breaking through the clouds. Her hands slid up to grasp his shoulders. She was shivery and breathless, hot and cold all at once. His tongue traced her lips and she hazily recalled his explanation. *The parties involved open their mouths.*

She parted her lips, and felt him smile. Tentatively, she opened her mouth wider. His tongue dipped inside, tasting her. Then their tongues met, and she nearly gasped aloud from the sensation. It was her first sip of champagne, the delight of galloping over fields, the force of a summer storm—all rolled into one. This. This was kissing.

When he finally lifted his head, she blinked. Her senses swam, so that she had to clutch at his shoulders to remain upright. His hands remained at her waist, and she was not inclined to ask him to remove them.

"Have I answered your question?" he asked, a crooked half- smile on his face.

"Yes. That was…most satisfactory."

And dizzying, and intoxicating. She hoped she wasn't staring up at him too foolishly. He let out a low breath and released her.

"I've kept you from your duties long enough," he said.

"Yes." She removed her hands from his shoulders, but couldn't make herself step away from him. "Well… I should be going. Thank you for the education, sir."

"Anna." The sound of her name on his lips made her heart give a curious little leap. "Call me Jonathan, please. And if you have any further questions about matters of this nature, please don't hesitate to ask. I'd gladly assist your understanding." There was a definite twinkle in his eyes now.

"I will, sir. Jonathan." Warmth sifted through her entire body. "Good afternoon."

"It's been a most delightful one. Until next time, Anna."

She did not bob a curtsey this time, only turned and went up the path. Just before she entered the dairy, she glanced back to see him leaning against the sun-dappled wall. His arms were crossed, and he was watching her with a strangely rueful smile.

***

The next morning, Giles was still asleep when she entered his bedchamber. As instructed, she opened the drapes, then went to stir up the banked coals. When she turned from that task, she saw he had woken and was sitting up against the ornate headboard of his bed. Again, the sheets had fallen to reveal an expanse of male skin—but somehow his shoulders did not look quite so broad, his chest so firm as they had the day before.

No matter. His eyes were still blue, his features as handsome as ever.

"Good morning, Anna," he said. "Come over here."

She quickly obeyed, but when she stood beside the bed, ready to demonstrate her newfound knowledge, he shifted away.

"Sit beside me." He patted the coverlet. "Don't be shy."

Anna slid onto the bed. Why, it was almost as if they had woken together—as they would once they were married. How agreeable of him to give her an early taste of that life.

Her legs pressed against his, and she could feel the warmth of sleep still clinging to his skin. He took her hands, his fingers stroking her palms.

"Why, you're chilled my dear. Let me warm you."

Before she could say that the hearth would be heating the

room soon, he pulled her against him. She sprawled against his chest in a most unbecoming way.

"Are you comfortable?" he asked.

"Actually, I'd rather—"

"Let's try this. You sit atop me."

"I... what?"

"Astride."

She stared at him. What he was suggesting was outrageous!

Then again, there was so much she didn't know about intimate relations. He had said he would show her, so she must be willing to learn. This was her future husband, after all. Slowly, she sat up.

"Very good," he said. "Yes, that's it. Lift your dress and climb on me. One leg to either side."

She lifted her skirts, exposing her legs most shockingly. "Like this?" It did not seem at all the thing.

"Yes, yes, just so. Now slide forward a bit... ahh."

There was an odd lump beneath the covers, just where she was sitting. Did the poor man have some sort of condition?

"Are you well?" she asked. "I'm not hurting you, am I?"

"No, not at all. You're performing your duties most excellently."

She adjusted her skirts, trying to cover herself, but he shook his head.

"Let me see you, Anna. You're quite lovely—no need to hide from me."

She supposed it was true. A husband and wife had nothing to conceal from one another, and certainly not once they were sharing the same bed. Giles was merely getting an early peek.

He folded her skirts back, until her legs were entirely bared. Smiling, he began to run his hands up and down her thighs. Each stroke ended closer to the edge of her drawers, where a peculiar, throbbing heat was beginning to build.

"You've shapely legs," he said. "Let me see your arms."

Feeling vaguely like a horse being assessed by a buyer, she pushed her sleeves up and held her arms out for his inspection. "Here they are."

"No, no." He laughed. "I must view your entire arm. Take your dress off from the shoulder."

It was a very improper command. Then again, everything here was improper: she was alone with him, in his bed, sitting atop him, with her legs exposed. Revealing her shoulders certainly could not make matters any worse. She pushed down the sudden impulse to hop off the bed and flee the room.

Slowly, she pulled down one shoulder of her dress and slipped her arm free, then repeated the action on the other side. She had not been able to bear the cloth of her maid's costume against her bare skin and had, perhaps unwisely, brought her finely embroidered shift. She was careful to don it only when Martha's back was turned. No one would see it beneath her dress. No one except Giles. She clutched her dress, so that it would not slip down.

"Still so modest?" He shook his head. "It won't do. Lift your arms above your head."

"But... my dress will fall."

"Exactly." His smile was predatory.

It was shocking, to hear him speak so. To have his avid gaze fastened on her, as if she were a bon-bon ready to be devoured. True, he had a reputation as a rake, but until now she had not quite understood what that meant. But this was Giles, who had smuggled her love notes and arranged to meet with her secretly. She should not feel so reluctant. After all, weren't they on the verge of an understanding?

Unclasping her fingers, she let the dress fall, then lifted her arms. He made a low sound in his throat, his eyes moving to her breasts.

Then his hands went there as well, and she nearly stopped breathing. The thin fabric of her shift did little to protect her from the heat of his touch. He cupped her, his palms brushing against her nipples. Her breasts tightened, pressing against the cloth, and he took the tips in his fingers. Fiery sensations sped through her as he fondled her. He began moving beneath her, rocking her up and down, while his breath came faster. Faster.

She felt giddy. The lump beneath the covers rubbed against her in a strangely satisfying way. There was an ache at her center—a yearning that spread through her entire body. She felt like she was stretching wings she'd never known she'd had.

Giles let out a yelp and fell back against the pillows. He lay there without moving, one arm flung across his face, though she could see the satisfied smile on his lips.

"Excellent work, Anna," he said, without removing his arm from in front of his eyes. "You may go."

What? She was dismissed, just like that? The sensations inside her began to ebb, leaving a restless dissatisfaction behind. Awkwardly, she climbed off the bed. She slipped her arms through her sleeves, then shook down her skirts, her throat dry with disappointment.

Then he levered himself up on his elbows and smiled at

her. "I'll see you tomorrow morning, of course. Good day, Anna."

That smile, so warm and intimate, lifted some of the unhappiness from her lungs. She mustn't be so downhearted, just because their encounter hadn't been quite what she had expected. Obviously there was a great deal for her to learn.

All of this would be easier if she didn't have to continue her disguise—but clearly Giles was enjoying the deception. She supposed he wasn't troubled at the thought of being found out. If that happened, all he would need to do was propose to her immediately. Scandalous gossip would reach London, of course, but their marriage would still all but the fiercest tongues.

Though her mother would be upset, once she found out the particular details of Anna's adventures.... A surge of guilt accompanied the thought, but Anna pushed it away.

Certainly Giles was going to propose soon. There was nothing to fear.

It wasn't until she was descending the narrow servant's stairs that she realized he hadn't kissed her. After the trouble she'd gone to, for nothing! Well. She would just have to make sure that tomorrow, they kissed.

Anna leaned against the fence near the stables, idly weaving grass-stems between her fingers. She had nearly forgotten it was her half-day, until Mrs. Foutch had shooed her out of the parlor while she was dusting. Now she had the entire afternoon free. Originally, she had thought to walk the few miles to the Caswell's and secretly meet with Belinda, to gossip and giggle over Giles and her own daring disguise. Yet, somehow, she didn't have the heart for it.

Instead, her feet had taken her out the kitchen door and through the gate. Past the dairy and the brick wall where Jonathan had shown her what a true kiss was. She had fetched up at the stables, an odd restlessness running through her.

If she were Anna Harcourt, instead of Anna the maid, she would direct one of the grooms to saddle a mount for her. She'd head for the open fields and let the wind against her face cool her impatience. Ah, she missed her gray mare, Isolde.

But there was Windsor—she could not mistake that impressively large black shape—being led from the stables. She leaned forward... but no, the man with him was not Jonathan. They entered the ring, where the groom began to put Windsor through his paces. The horse had a wonderfully fluid gait. No wonder Giles had purchased him.

She wandered closer, the scent of sweet clover in the fields mixing with hay and earthy manure. When she reached the fence surrounding the ring, she realized someone else was standing in the shadows, watching the horse.

Jonathan.

Her stomach tickled, as though she had swallowed a bee, and she hesitated.

"Miss Anna." He glanced over at her, as though he'd been aware of her presence all along. "Join me?"

"Good afternoon, Jonathan," she said, coming to stand beside him. "Are you making sure Windsor is behaving?"

He smiled, as though her use of his given name pleased him. "He is, now that the stable-boys know how clever he can be at slipping out of his stall."

"Why aren't you working with Windsor? Aren't you in charge of him?"

"Not any longer." He sounded displeased.

Curiosity pricked her—but it wasn't her place to ask what had happened. He turned back to watch the horse, and she studied him covertly. His jaw was set, his lips firm, but she knew how soft and coaxing they could be...

Drat. Why was she thinking of such things, when she loved Giles? And he loved her in return—of course he did. Why, just look at how intimate he had been with her this morning.

Then why had it not felt quite like love?

Letting out a sigh, she rested her folded arms on the top rail. This adventure of hers was becoming rather too complicated.

"Have you ever done something you regretted?" she asked.

Jonathan looked at her, and she caught her breath at the intensity of his gaze. "Why do you ask?" he said. "Are you sorry about our kiss yesterday?"

"No! Not at all." She dropped her eyes to the buttons of his coat. How thoughtless of her. "That is... I didn't mean to imply..."

There was a subtle self-mockery in his voice. "Indeed, of all the things I regret, that kiss is certainly not one of them."

She peeked up at him. "You are very skilled—have no fears on that account."

He laughed, sudden and bright, and the shadow of sorrow left his face. "I'm glad you think so. But tell me, Anna. What's troubling you?"

For a foolish moment, she nearly confided everything to him. But then he would know she was more than a maid, and the easy companionability between them would freeze and break. Jonathan was the only person at Wildering Hall she felt at all comfortable with, and she would not put that in jeopardy.

"I'm beginning to think I've misjudged a situation," she said.

It wasn't until she put the feeling into words that she realized it was true. She did not know exactly what was wrong between herself and Giles, only that something was.

Jonathan looked at her closely. "Then you're probably right. I've found that those kinds of suspicions often prove correct."

She nodded, grateful that he was not pressing for details. "It's just that—I'm a bit impulsive, you see."

"Are you?" There was dry humor in his tone. "I wouldn't have guessed."

"I don't go about kissing gentlemen every day, I'd have you know." She narrowed her eyes at him, but she was no good at pretending to be in a temper when she truly was not.

"Yes, it was a special case—I understand that." His expression sobered, and he reached for her hand. His fingers were warm against hers. "Anna, is there anything I can do to help you?"

Just being near his solid, sympathetic presence was helping tremendously. He was right—she should heed her intuition. Tomorrow morning she would ask Giles straight out if he was merely toying with her affections. And if he was? She couldn't bear thinking of it, not now. Tomorrow would come soon enough.

She looked up at Jonathan. "You've already done a great deal, and I thank you for it."

"If you need anything from me, don't hesitate to ask. If

you can't find me, the stable-hands will direct you."

It was kind of him to offer, though she didn't know what a groom could do to aid her in the event she required assistance. Still, it made happiness curl through her that he would try.

And she must admit, he had an air of competency—even command—about him.

"Were you in the army?" The question popped out before she had time to consider it.

"No. Why do you ask?"

"No reason." Not one that she could confess, at any rate.

She stared at their clasped hands. It felt so natural to touch him, yet exciting too. Comforting and delicious, like a pot of chocolate. It was a whimsical notion, comparing Jonathan to hot chocolate—yet somehow fitting.

From the ring, Windsor gave a sharp whinny, and Jonathan straightened.

"Forgive me," he said. "I must speak with the stable-boy." He did not, however, release her hand.

"Of course. Thank you for the conversation."

He gently squeezed her fingers. "I hope to see you tomorrow, Anna. Look for me here."

"I will."

Watching his broad shoulders as he walked away, she could not help thinking what a well-made man he was. Oh, and what a contrary goose she was! Of the two men she planned to speak with tomorrow, she was most eager to see the servant, and not the master.

Belinda would be shocked, but somehow Anna could not regret it. The only worrisome thing was, what if Giles did not love her after all? The thought made her stomach knot with dread. She would have to leave the Wildering's mansion immediately.

Would she ever see Jonathan again? The thought was a pin stabbed into her heart.

***

Anna had opened the drapes, coaxed the coals back to life, refilled the ewer, and still Giles slept. Well. She must wake him—and she knew just how. First, a kiss. And then, her question.

He lay in the center of the big bed, with barely enough room for her to lie beside him. In slumber, his face looked soft. Nothing like Jonathan's rugged features. But still quite handsome, of course. She bent and pressed her lips to his.

Giles gave a somewhat ungentlemanly snort, but his eyes did not open. His lips, however, began to move hungrily against hers. Then his arms came about her. Remembering what she had learned, she opened her mouth. If kissing Jonathan had been lovely, how much sweeter would it be with Giles?

Surely that wave of pleasure would wash over her at any moment. She pressed against Giles, waiting. When he swept his tongue into her mouth, she was ready—but where was that bright, dizzying sensation?

Perhaps she needed a little more time to become accustomed to his kiss. It was pleasant enough, if a bit sloppy, and she did like the feel of his hands roaming over her shoulders. He pushed the sleeves of her dress down, baring her collarbone. Then he tugged harder, exposing her breasts and pinning her arms to her sides with the fabric.

His hands were eager on her breasts, his mouth ferocious against hers, and she felt warmth begin to tingle through her. Still, she had a question to ask him. She broke the kiss, though he still held her tightly.

"Wait," she said. "I must know—"

"Not now," he said. "Lift your skirts. I must have you."

"But—"

"Anna, you are driving me mad. Quickly, now." His hands were insistent, his face flushed.

Desire for her was printed on those handsome features, yet she hesitated. She was beginning to understand that desire was not the same thing as love. And a kiss was not an answer.

"Don't you think we ought to... wait?" she asked.

"Wait for what?" He took a handful of her dress and hauled it up.

"Well..." She took a deep breath and pushed her skirts back down. "Until after the wedding."

"The wedding?" He looked at her blankly. "Oh. My congratulations on your upcoming nuptials. But surely you aren't a—"

"*Our* wedding, Giles!" She pulled away and stared at him. "Don't you love me, at least a little?"

His look of shock quickly gave way to disdain. "Love you? By god, you think that I'd marry you, just because I invited you into my bed? Stupid girl, to look so far above your station. You're only a maid with a pretty face."

Each word was a knife stabbing into her. Terrible, terrible, the knowledge of her own blindness and stupidity.

Giles had never recognized her. Did he even know that Miss Harcourt's given name was Anna? He had no idea who she was. He thought her a servant!

Fury and mortification blazed through her. She leaped off the bed and grabbed the ewer of water on the nightstand.

"Why, you're nothing but a rake!" she cried. "How could you? You... you're contemptible!"

Wrapping both hands around the ewer, she flung the water over him. It made a satisfying splash, and an even better sight—Giles soaking wet and spluttering in his now-damp sheets.

"You're sacked!" he yelled. "No pay—and don't ever let me see your face again."

As if he would even recognize it.

"Gladly." Anna threw the ewer down on the carpet.

"Go—and send Martha to me at once."

Without bothering to reply, Anna turned and stalked out of Giles' bedroom. She made sure to slam the door loudly behind her.

It took a moment for her to realize she was shaking. What a dreadful affair. Anger and shame chased through her—hot, then icy, then hot again.. She could never let anyone know what had happened. And she must depart Wildering Hall at once.

Holding her head high, Anna found Mrs. Foutch in the blue parlor and informed her that she was leaving service immediately. She did not give any further details, but the housekeeper gave her a sharp look. Even if the woman suspected the truth of the matter, there was very little she could do about it.

"Very well," Mrs. Foutch said, after a long pause. "I'm afraid I can't give you a reference. Fetch your things and go."

Anna did not argue, though had she been a maid in truth she would have been in desperate straits. She stumbled once on the narrow stairs to the servant's quarters, barking her shin. The sharp pain was a welcome distraction from the ache swirling inside her. What a fool she had been, imagining that her dreams were reality. She'd built an intricate castle of clouds, thinking it was solid and sure, and the wind had blown it to tatters.

"Watch yourself!" It was Martha, going down the stairs with an armful of linens. "How clumsy you are, Anna."

The girl's hostility made sense, now that Anna could see the situation clearly. Giles trifled with the maids. It was reprehensible and most ungentlemanly, but she had the uneasy feeling that it was not uncommon, either. Clearly, Martha fancied herself in love with the master, though she knew better than to expect any offer of legitimacy. Likely Giles gave her a trinket or two—but if the worst happened, that was hardly enough to keep the girl.

"Martha, wait a moment."

The red-haired maid scowled, but paused. "What is it? I've work to do."

"I'm leaving. The master has asked for you to attend him in his chamber."

The smile blossoming on Martha's face made her look almost beautiful. "Has he now? I must go, directly."

"Wait." Anna set her hand on the other girl's arm. "If… if you should ever find yourself in need of assistance, go to Caswell Hall and ask for Belinda. Tell her that Anna the maid sent you."

Martha seemed well enough, now, but any number of troubles could arise for her. Not every maid could simply leave and resume her role as the daughter of gentility. Guilt scratched just under Anna's skin.

"I don't need any help from you," Martha said. "Goodbye." She pushed past without a backward glance.

Well, Anna had done her best. Her throat tight, she gathered up the few items she had borrowed from Belinda's maid. She was glad to leave the narrow cot and cramped quarters under the eaves, the dreadfully early hours, the difficult work—but the relief was buried under a thick layer of humiliation. She had been so idiotically certain of herself. And ultimately, so very wrong. The knowledge was bitter in her mouth.

On her way out of the kitchen, Cook gave her a rueful smile and handed her small bundle of food.

"Good luck, dearie," she said.

The simple kindness was nearly enough to unleash the torrent of tears Anna felt building behind her eyes.

"Thank you," she managed, tucking the food into her bag.

Not yet—she would not cry yet. She must go by the stables and say farewell to Jonathan. Blinking fiercely, she left the kitchen gardens behind. The wall where they had kissed— no, she could not look at it. The dairy, the fields filled with clover.

Outside the stables, she paused to take a shaky breath. What would she tell him? Her mother was ill… yes. That would explain why she must go so quickly, and why she was overset.

She had no chance, however, to use her lie. When she asked for Jonathan, the other grooms shook their heads, saying he had not arrived yet. She could not pen him a note, so she asked only that they inform him she had left service. At least he would know she had gone.

There was no way to convey to him how highly she thought of him, after only a few days' acquaintance—or how much she suspected she would miss him.

Sniffing, she turned her back on the Wildering's estate and began the long walk to the Caswell's. By the time she reached the main road, she could not contain her tears. She blinked fiercely, but hot moisture trickled down her cheeks. However would she explain to Belinda what had happened? She clutched her bundle tightly against her chest and, head bowed, kept on.

Hoof-beats made her glance up to see a rider approaching. She hurried to the side of the road and stood there, eyes fixed on the dusty grasses, waiting for the traveler to pass by.

They did not. The hoof-beats slowed, then stopped as the rider came to a halt beside her.

"Anna?"

She looked up in surprise, to see Jonathan regarding her.

"Oh. Hello, Jonathan."

She could not say it was lovely to see him—though a part of her heart lightened with gladness to hear his voice again. But it was clear she had been crying, and she had never been a pretty weeper. Her cheeks and nose were certainly flushed, her eyes red-rimmed—not the best face to present to the world.

"Were you coming to find me?" There was a concerned note in his voice. In one fluid movement, he slid off his horse, holding the reins loosely in one hand.

"No—though I did look for you at the stables. I… I've left the Wildering's employ."

He regarded her closely. "And not happily, I see. What happened?"

"I'd rather not say." There was no earthly way she could confess the magnitude of her folly to Jonathan. He would think so poorly of her, if he knew.

"Ah, Anna..."

He opened his arms, and somehow it was the most natural thing in the world for her to step into his embrace. She pressed her tear-stained face against his coat, smelling wool and horse and Jonathan. The feel of his arms around her was safety and sympathy—and it made her start crying again.

One hand smoothing her hair, Jonathan made sounds that she suspected he used to soothe restive horses. Nevertheless, she found herself comforted.

At last she had no more tears. She gave a final sniff and looked up at him. There was a curious expression in his eyes, a rueful tenderness that surprised her.

"Have you a handkerchief?" he asked.

When she shook her head, he pulled one from his waistcoat pocket and gave it to her. She dried her eyes, then turned away to blow her nose. After that, she couldn't offer it back to him, so she stuffed his kerchief into her apron pocket.

"Well." She gave him a smile that wobbled at the corners. "I shouldn't keep you—you were headed for the stables, I presume?"

"The stables can wait. Where are you bound, Anna? Have you a place to go? Friends, family?"

"Yes." She could tell him nothing more, despite the questioning look on his face.

He waited a moment, clearly expecting her to say more. Finally, when she did not, he cleared his throat. "Then, wherever you need to go, I will take you there."

"I couldn't ask you to!" Indeed, she could not imagine

arriving home with one of the Wildering's grooms as her escort.

"You don't need to ask. I will help you, Anna."

It was clear he was not going to let her continue walking alone down the road. "Very well. You may accompany me to Caswell Hall. I've... friends there who can give me further assistance."

He gave her a close look. "You'll continue in service, then? Is there a place for you there?"

"I believe so." Not, however, in the servant's quarters.

She would resume her role as a visiting friend. Her parents already thought her in residence with the Caswells. When she had first arrived, she and Belinda had hidden her luggage and passed it off as a short visit. Belinda had promised to intercept any correspondence, and the initial letter concerning her fortnight's stay was concealed in the bottom of Belinda's jewelry-box. Luckily they hadn't simply tossed it away—it was time for her to arrive for her extended visit.

"I'll take you to Caswell Hall." He mounted again, as easily as he had dismounted, and held out his hand. "It will be faster this way. Come up—don't be afraid."

She took his hand. With his help, and by rather improperly lifting her skirts and stepping on his booted foot, she managed to get onto the horse. Jonathan settled her in front of him. He slipped one arm around her waist and pulled her gently back, until she was leaning against his broad chest.

"You're an unusual maid, Anna," he said.

"Oh, not at all. I'm quite the usual sort." She was glad he could not see her face. It was much easier to lie when she could avoid looking in his eyes.

His laughter vibrated through her. "I don't know of many maids who ride, or speak with the accent of the gentry."

"I was fortunate in my education."

"Or proposition men for kissing lessons."

Heat blazed into her cheeks. "It was a special circumstance. Really, must you keep bringing it up?" She had learned her lesson, and a painful one it had been.

"Yes. You are unforgettable, Anna." He dipped his head and spoke softly, his breath warming the side of her neck. "Might I come visit you at Caswell Hall?"

"No!" The word was out before she could think.

He pulled back, and the arm about her waist stiffened. "I had thought—well, never mind. My apologies if I've offended you."

She wanted to turn and press her lips against his. She wanted to tell him that he had not been wrong. They shared a mutual admiration that, in any other circumstance, could easily have blossomed past friendship into something nearly as bright as the sun.

But she could not tell him, because it was all built on a lie. It was better to let him think she did not care for him, since any kind of future between them was simply impossible.

So she held her tongue, and the remainder of the ride to the Caswell's estate passed in unhappy silence. Jonathan guided his mount up the long drive and around to the servant's entrance. When she would have slid down, he held her tightly against him for a moment.

"Goodbye, sweet Anna." He leaned forward and kissed her cheek, and she wanted to weep again.

He helped her dismount, and she could not meet his eyes. It was only when she had reached the door that she had enough control over her emotions to turn and look at him. He was every maid—and maiden's—dream, with his strong features and keen eyes, his hair roughened by the wind. But she had learned not to trust her dreams.

"Farewell, Jonathan," she said. "I will never forget you, either."

Before he could say anything, she whirled and went into Caswell Hall, shutting the door firmly behind her.

***

"Anna!" Belinda jumped up from her window-seat, her fair curls bobbing, and rushed to enfold Anna in a lily-scented embrace. "I simply can't accustom myself to seeing you dressed as a maid. Is it your half-day? Has Giles proposed yet? Oh, come sit and tell me everything."

"There's not much to tell. I've left the Wildering's for good."

Belinda's blue eyes widened. "Heavens—and after all our planning, too. Were you found out?"

"No." If only it were that simple. "In fact, I was not recognized at all. By anyone."

"But… not even by Giles?" Belinda took her hands and clasped them tightly. "Oh, dear. I thought he loved you. How could he not see past a maid's cap and apron?"

"I was mistaken about him." Dreadfully mistaken—though the clues had been there, if only she had been wise enough to see them. "It's for the best, really. Giles and I wouldn't suit."

Not when she knew he didn't truly see a person, merely a conquest. Their secret meetings, his endearments to her, they had been empty. He had not wanted to marry her, only take advantage of her. She sighed.

"Well—no harm done," Belinda said. "And now you've a daring adventure in your past, to lend you a worldly air."

A worldly air, indeed. Anna had learned more than she'd wanted, and the price of that wisdom had tarnished her view of the world. She wouldn't mar Belinda's innocence by revealing everything. At least, not while the knowledge was still painfully tender.

"I'm afraid the life of a servant is nothing to wax poetic about, Bel. Only five days and my hands are chapped from scrubbing. And I'd be happy never to observe the sun rising again."

Belinda sprang up. "That's all behind you now. This way you'll be here for our country ball! We must arrange for you to 'arrive' immediately. Here—I've hidden your gown in the back of my wardrobe. You change, and I'll manage the details."

An hour later, Anna Harcourt rode up to the front gates of Caswell Manor in a carriage stacked with her luggage. She presented the letter from her parents to the elder Caswells, apologized for the sudden arrival, and was welcomed warmly. Only she and Belinda knew that, folded in the depths of her valise, lay a plain maid's dress. The last evidence of her ill-fated adventure as a maid.

Well—not quite the last. She had kept Jonathan's handkerchief. There were initials embroidered in the corner, but she had not wanted to call Belinda's attention to it. She'd tucked the kerchief, crumpled and still a bit soggy, into her reticule for later examination.

It was not difficult to plead fatigue after luncheon, and retire to her room. She really was quite exhausted, but first…

Sitting on her bed, Anna unfolded the square of linen. It was hemmed quite precisely, and in one corner, worked in green silk, were the letters *J.A.* Jonathan what? She didn't even know his last name. Abercrombie? Aiken? Who had embroidered those well-stitched initials? A sister? A wife?

No. Not a wife. She lay back against the pillows, weaving the kerchief between her fingers. Jonathan was not like Giles. Despite having been very mistaken in her judgments recently, she felt the truth in this. There was a quiet integrity about Jonathan. If he were married, she was quite certain he wouldn't go about kissing other ladies. Or comforting them, or escorting them wherever they needed to go.

A breath, not quite a sob, escaped her lips. She brought the kerchief to her nose, but there was no trace of his scent.

Perhaps… mightn't she don her maid's clothing and go return his kerchief? The thought lodged itself under her ribs, painful and exciting all at once.

Then the weight of wisdom settled down on her. Returning to the Wildering's estate and seeing Jonathan again, however briefly, was a terrible idea. There was nothing to be gained by it but more heartache.

She slipped the handkerchief under her pillow. It could lend sweetness to her dreams, but that was all.

***

A week after her arrival, Caswell Manor hummed with excitement. The country ball was to be held that evening. The Caswells were, as usual, quite generous. They had invited all the local gentry, even the minor squires.

Belinda was elated—but then, she was always one to

enjoy a party. As Anna herself had been, until lately.

"Oh, Anna," her friend said, "we'll have so much fun tonight! It's nothing like the grand London events, but that's part of what makes it so amusing. We can drink champagne instead of over-sweetened lemonade, and dance with whomever we please. And the conversation…" She fell back, laughing, on her bed.

Anna waited patiently for her friend to catch her breath. "The conversation?"

"Last year, the vicar and Squire Brown, one of the local farmers, got into a heated discussion about different kinds of fertilizers. You could hear them shouting about manures, even over the music. Oh, and there was the time Miss Landry smuggled her pet pig into the ball, and it got loose during the dancing. Some of the ladies squealed as loudly as the pig!"

"Oh, my." Anna joined in her friend's laughter. She had not laughed in too long—it felt like a bubble of air had formed in her chest and was finally escaping. "Then I am eagerly awaiting the evening's festivities."

"Which ball-gown are you going to wear?" Belinda sat up. "The green silk is quite becoming on you—and I have just the ornament for your hair."

"Is it a pig?"

"Yes, a very small one." Belinda laughed and shook her head. "I'm so pleased to see you out of your melancholy, Anna. Tonight will be splendid. I promise."

That promise had yet to prove true, however.

Anna stood with Belinda as the Caswells received their guests. It was not as tedious as the usual receiving lines, though, especially with Belinda poking her in the ribs and telling her to watch for smuggled-in livestock.

"Mr. Giles Wildering, Mrs. Wildering," the butler announced.

Cold squeezed Anna's chest. Oh, no! Had she considered it, she would have realized that of course Giles and his mother would be in attendance. She shot Belinda a panicked look, but her friend only gave her a reassuring smile.

If only she could creep back behind one of the potted palms in the hallway... too late. Belinda's mother was greeting Giles. In a moment she would turn and present their houseguest. There was no escape. Anna pasted a smile across her face, and prayed he would not suddenly recognize her.

"Miss Harcourt." Giles bowed over her gloved hand.

When he looked up, his charming smile faltered for a moment. Anna contrived her haughtiest expression.

"Mr. Wildering," she said, keeping her voice cool and even, with no hint of their past history. "A pleasure to see you again."

"Ah, yes." His smile was firmly back in place. "I recall our lovely interlude in the Benning's rose arbor. Perhaps you will take a stroll about the gardens with me, this evening?"

"Perhaps." Never.

"If you grace me with your company, it will be the highlight of the ball." He pitched his voice for her ears alone. "I've missed you dreadfully."

He pressed her fingers between his own, and it was all Anna could do not to snatch her hand away. What a rogue. She could not imagine how she had been so blind.

"Come along, Giles," his mother said, taking his arm. "I believe I see the Earl of Blakely. His niece is a lovely girl, if you recall."

With a final, burning glance at her, he let his mother tow

him into the crowd. Anna wished she had something to sip, to wash the taste of his presence from her mouth.

"I hear the music beginning," Belinda's mother said. "Why don't you girls go enjoy the dancing? Almost all our guests have arrived—you needn't keep us company here any longer."

"Thank you, Mama." Belinda dropped a kiss on her mother's cheek. "I think Anna is in need of refreshment."

Her father gave them a stern look, though there was a twinkle in his eye. "Mind the champagne, Belinda. I don't want to find you sitting in the hall again, giggling to no one."

"Don't fret," Belinda said. "I have Anna to giggle with this year." She grinned at her parents, then linked arms with Anna and led her away.

"I can't believe the Wilderings are here," Anna said. "Now I'll have to avoid Giles for the entire evening."

"And he still never recognized you." Belinda shook her head. "Come, let's get some champagne and tell secrets. Surely you have a secret or two. Don't dissemble. I can see it in your face, Anna."

There were things she could never share with Belinda. Luckily, there were a few tidbits she had discovered in her short tenure as a maid.

Anna leaned close to her friend. "Giles Wildering's coats are all padded at the shoulders. He's really rather small of stature." She had her suspicions about his breeches as well.

"Never say so!" Belinda tipped her eyes up to the ceiling. "He's nothing but lies, isn't he?"

Anna took a sip of her champagne. "Now you tell me a secret."

"I'm thinking of bribing one of the footmen to bring a

chicken in." Belinda's smile was full of mischief.

"You're incorrigible."

"Oh listen, it's the quadrille!" Belinda set down her champagne flute. "I'll dance with Jaded Giles if you promise to find someone exciting to dance with."

"I've had a bit too much excitement in my life, recently," Anna said.

"You mustn't let me make this sacrifice in vain." Belinda affected a martyred expression. "Please, Anna. I want you to enjoy yourself, to dance."

Anna never could resist her friend's pleading. "Very well. But you must make sure Giles is well in hand before I step onto the floor."

"Don't take too long." Belinda waggled her gloved fingers, then vanished into the crowd.

Anna took another swallow of champagne. Truly, she had no heart for dancing—but she *had* promised. To dance, at any rate. Enjoying herself was out of the question. She glanced about for the most uninteresting prospect she could find. There—one of the local squire's sons, a gangly fellow who flushed when she smiled at him.

Still, the lad was enough up to scratch that a moment later he approached and asked her to join him in the quadrille. Anna accepted, making sure to guide them to the second line, where they would have no chance of coming face-to-face with Belinda and her partner.

She caught snatches of conversation as they moved through the figures of the dance. Behind her, Mrs. Wildering was exclaiming to someone about the unreliability of country servants and their questionable references. Anna was quite certain she was the cause of that particular complaint.

Soon enough, the dance was ended. She thanked the squire's son and retreated back to her corner, where Belinda soon joined her.

"Heavens, Giles Wildering's hands like to roam," she said. "I had to swat him with my fan twice. And then he wouldn't stop talking about his new horse."

"His horse?" It must be Windsor, surely.

"Well, his *former* new horse. Apparently the man who sold it to him changed his mind. Mr. Wildering was quite vexed."

Anything that vexed him, Anna found quite pleasing. "Who sold him the horse? I'll have to thank the gentleman."

"It was Sir Averly, I believe. He breeds horses—and look, there he is now. Late, but at least he came. He's far and away the most interesting gentleman in the area. You should dance with him, Anna. Come, I'll introduce you."

As they moved across the dance floor, the back of Anna's neck began to prickle. Belinda was leading her toward a tall, sandy-haired figure that was suddenly, achingly, familiar. Surely it couldn't be. It was a passing resemblance, that was all. She tried to calm her pounding heart.

Then the man turned. His rugged features were unmistakable. Those penetrating green eyes fixed on her face and surprise flashed across his expression, quickly masked.

"Sir Averly," Belinda said. "How lovely that you could attend our ball."

"Indeed." His gaze had not left Anna's.

"Allow me to introduce my friend, Miss Anna Harcourt. She's currently a guest at Caswell Hall. Anna, meet Sir Jonathan Avery."

"Sir." Anna could scarcely breathe.

Jonathan. Here—and somehow a member of the gentry.

It unbalanced her completely. She was surprised the walls hadn't begun to cave in on her.

"Miss Harcourt, it's a pleasure to make your acquaintance. Would you care to further it by strolling with me on the terrace?" He held out his arm to her.

Belinda blinked, then leaned her head close to Anna's. "Go on," she whispered. "He's a gentleman—you've no cause to worry."

"Thank you." Anna found her voice. "I'd be delighted."

She placed her hand on his arm. The feel of his strength under her fingers reminded her of how it felt to be wrapped in his embrace. Heat flushed into her cheeks and she kept her gaze resolutely fixed on the French doors ahead.

Neither of them spoke until they had gained the low balustrade at the edge of the terrace. Then she released his arm and turned to face him. Light spilling from the ballroom left half his face in shadow. It was difficult to tell if he were pleased to see her, or angry. Or both.

"So," she said, her voice a touch unsteady. "You are not a stable-hand."

"And you are not a maid—though I suspected as much upon our first meeting."

"You did?" How mortifying, that her disguise had been so easy to see through. "What gave me away?"

"No country maid ever spoke so elegantly, for one thing. And it was quite a stretch to imagine such a lovely maid having no experience in the arts of love. Unless, of course, you came from a much more sheltered existence."

"Yet you said nothing." He had known, all along. A curious sense of relief washed through her.

"What could I say? You had your reasons for your

charade. It was not my place to press you for them. And... I was selfish."

She tilted her head. In the half-light she could just make out the rueful smile she'd seen before on his face.

"Selfish?"

"If I pretended you were not a lady of refinement, then I could continue meeting you." One hand came up to cup her cheek. "I could kiss you, without restraint or consequence. I didn't want to lose you, Anna."

A thrill went through her. When he dropped his hand from her face, she took his fingers in hers.

"You let me think that you were simply a groom, in order to continue our acquaintance. But why were you so often at the Wildering's?"

"Giles Wildering wanted to buy Windsor. I was not wholly in accord with the idea, so decided to keep an eye on matters."

No doubt Giles had thought that such a big black horse would enhance his manliness. "I heard that you changed your mind about the purchase."

"Almost immediately. You are the only reason I didn't turn back with Windsor at once. When you were gone, there was no reason to linger."

"Are you... angry with me?"

"Why?" His hand tightened around hers.

"I deceived you."

He gave a quiet laugh. "Not very well."

"I thought I would never see you again." Her heart was sore with joy.

"Ah, Anna."

He stepped forward, and somehow she was in his arms

again. It felt like home.

"You won't tell, will you?" she asked. "Anyone?"

"All your secrets are safe with me. I only ask one thing."

"A kiss?" She pressed hopefully against him.

"A lifetime of kisses. Anna Harcourt, I won't lose you again. Will you allow me to call upon you?"

Her battered heart was suddenly, gloriously, whole again. The happiness that had been missing now sparked through her entire body, leaving her breathless. Her spirit was light as air. Lighter.

"Yes, Jonathan. Oh, most certainly yes!"

He dipped his head then, and their lips met in a kiss full of promise and desire. Giddy with happiness, Anna held on to him. There was nothing but this perfect moment, stretching into the future.

The sweet night wind. The taste of her beloved. The brilliant, whirling stars.

~THE END~

Anthea Lawson

Kisses & Rogues

The Piano Tutor

"**M**y lady." The butler tapped at Diana Waverly's half-open door. "The piano tutor is here." He hesitated, a furrow marring his usually placid brow.

"Well, it *is* Wednesday." Diana laid her last black dress in the trunk she had been filling, then carefully closed the lid. "Tell Samantha it's time for her lesson. I'll be down directly."

The butler remained in the doorway, shifting his weight from foot to foot. "Forgive me, my lady, but it ... er, it is not the customary piano tutor. It is an altogether different gentleman."

She blinked. "But—Mr. Bent is Samantha's tutor. We have no other."

"I tried to tell him as much, but the gentleman insists."

Diana stood, frowning. "I'll see to him." They had few callers—the inevitable result of turning down a season's worth of invitations—and never unannounced visitors.

Tucking up a stray auburn curl, she started down the hallway toward the wide second floor landing. Mr. Bent had said nothing of this. He was quite reliable—if a bit dour to be tutoring a girl still recovering from the loss of her father.

At the top of the stairs she halted, pulled from her thoughts by the sound of music pouring from the parlor below. Someone very skilled was playing the piano.

She rested her hand on the mahogany banister and listened. Note after note tumbled through the entryway, reverberating between the high ceiling and marble floors. Sunlight streamed through the landing windows, making the dust motes swirl and glitter like gilded dancers.

Her stepdaughter Samantha joined her, her wiry twelve-year old body leaning over the railing. "I didn't know Mr. Bent could actually *play* the piano."

"It's not Mr. Bent." That much was clear, though who it might be and why he was in her parlor was a mystery Diana could not fathom.

She descended the stairs, the music growing fuller and more present with every step. She paused a moment at the parlor door, then, with a fortifying breath, went in. The instant she crossed the threshold, the music ceased. The magic that had been spilling into the house folded in upon itself and disappeared.

But its source remained—a broad-shouldered man with brown hair and intelligent grey eyes. He stood when he saw her and bowed with an easy grace.

"My lady."

She studied the stranger. Handsome, undeniably, with those compelling eyes and a smile that seemed genuine. He looked nothing like the stoop shouldered and outmoded Mr. Bent. For one thing, he was a good deal younger—he looked to be no more than a handful of years older than herself.

"Sir?" She hardly knew what to say. "Please explain yourself."

"Viscountess Merrowstone." The stranger's voice was rich and complex, the syllables of her title unexpectedly smooth to her ears. "Mr. Nicholas Jameson, at your service.

I've come to substitute for Mr. Bent, who has been called away unexpectedly."

"This is most irregular. I was not informed there was to be a replacement." She faced him squarely, ready to send him on his way. That was what she intended to do, but the words came out all wrong. "You play quite well."

He tipped his head, a smile lifting the corners of his mouth. "That would be a requirement, wouldn't it?"

"One would assume so." Though his bearing made her think he would be more suited to leaping a stallion over hedgerows than giving piano lessons to a twelve-year old. "You're quite certain you're a piano tutor?"

"Let me assure you of my qualifications." He extended an envelope. "I've a letter of recommendation from Lady Pembroke. You're acquainted, I believe?"

Diana nodded. Indeed, Lucy was a good friend, possessed of a generous spirit—though she was more than a little scandalous.

Henry had not approved of their friendship. Diana's gaze slipped past Mr. Jameson to the portrait of her late husband, Lord Henry Waverly, Viscount Merrowstone. His stern, formal features watched impassively, a cultivated remoteness in his expression. Solid and predictable in the portrait, just as in life. Lucy had annoyed him to no end.

Swallowing a sigh, Diana turned her attention to her friend's curling script.

Dearest Diana— I commend Mr. Nicholas Jameson to you as a piano tutor. He has provided my own Charlotte with lessons and has proven quite satisfactory. May I also point out—in case you had not noticed—that he is extremely handsome. He strikes me as a perfect diversion now that you have finally come out of mourning. I encourage you to take him on—in whatever capacities suit your needs. Pianists have such skilled hands.

She felt her cheeks burn as she glanced up at the gentleman in question. No doubt it had amused Lucy to have Mr. Jameson deliver such an outrageous "reference" in person.

"I see that she recommends you highly, sir," Diana said, biting her lip to avoid an embarrassed giggle. "I suppose we might consider having you." Oh dear, that hadn't sounded quite proper. She cleared her throat. "I mean *hiring* you. It wouldn't do to neglect Samantha's lessons while Mr. Bent is away."

"Oh, please hire him," Samantha said, peeking out from behind the doorway. She came in and stood on tiptoe to whisper in Diana's ear. "He seems ever so much nicer than Mr. Bent."

It was quite outside the regular course of things, yet there was no mistaking the eager note in Samantha's voice. No mistaking that Mr. Jameson was, as Lucy had mentioned, a very handsome man.

Her stepdaughter turned to him. "I heard you playing. It was marvelous! How do you do the part with your left hand? Could you show me?"

"Of course." He gave her an encouraging smile. "It's simple once you get the trick of it. Have you played any Mozart?"

"Oh yes!"

"Then you'll be able to master it easily. That is…." He raised a questioning brow at Diana.

"Oh very well," she said. "It appears you will be our replacement tutor until Mr. Bent returns." She ignored Samantha's muffled squeal. "Can you begin today?"

A spark leapt into his eyes. "Immediately."

Looking at him made heat creep into her cheeks. Despite herself, Lucy's advice rang in her head. As if she would consider something so scandalous as commencing an affair with the piano tutor. Really, her friend had no sense of propriety.

Samantha hurried to seat herself at the piano bench. "I'm ready!"

Diana was not sure whether she herself was ready, but events seemed to be carrying her along. She settled into the nearby wingback and straightened the rich indigo skirts of her new dress. It was odd to wear colors again. She had grown so accustomed to the solid black of mourning that she felt vulnerable without it. A part of her wanted to retreat back into its safety—but that was not fair to Samantha. Diana could not deny the hopeful light in the girl's eyes, the flash of her rare grin as she attempted to mimic Mr. Jameson's command of the keyboard.

As was customary during Samantha's lessons, Diana picked up her newest copy of *The Ladies' Monthly*, but the fashion plates held no interest for her. Her eyes kept wandering from the illustrations to steal quick glances at the new tutor—his long-fingered hands as he played a run of notes, the way his brown hair tumbled over his collar. More than once he seemed to sense her attention and she had to quickly drop her gaze back to the unseen pages.

The sound of his voice was so different from Mr. Bent's dry tones, and his praise and encouragement drew another flashing smile from Samantha. Something inside Diana uncoiled a notch, a deep tension she had not realized she had been carrying.

The shape of his muscular shoulders was barely concealed by the cut of his coat as he leaned forward to demonstrate some point. He radiated confidence and mastery. She imagined that everything he did would benefit from that focused energy.

From this angle he was in profile. His jaw was firm, his nose straight, his mouth strong, yet sensitive. She traced her own lips with a fingertip, then caught herself and hurriedly dropped her hand before he could notice.

Mr. Jameson turned to face her. "Will you?" he asked.

Diana's breath faltered as their gazes held a heartbeat too long. Clearly she had missed an important turn in the lesson while daydreaming.

"Sing for us," Samantha said, a touch of impatience in her voice. "Mr. Jameson has been showing me a marvelous pattern for accompanying songs, but I don't think I can sing and play at the same time."

Diana set aside her magazine. "Oh—I really couldn't. It's been so long." There didn't seem to be enough air in the room for her to breathe, let alone sing.

"Of course you can." Mr. Jameson's tone was assured. "Miss Samantha says you have a lovely singing voice." There was a challenge in his expression, as if he were curious to see what she would do.

"Please, Mama. Let's do *The Meeting of the Waters.*"

"Very well. If it's part of the lesson." She stood and took her place beside the piano, oddly reluctant to disappoint Mr. Jameson. Still, it had been a very long while. What if she had lost the knack altogether? "Samantha, you and Mr. Jameson must help by singing with me."

The piano tutor counted the tempo then signaled Samantha to begin. Diana took a deep breath and sang the first words. Mr. Jameson's rich baritone joined her, while her stepdaughter concentrated on the keyboard.

At first her alto sounded husky to her ears, the notes unsure. Soon enough, though, her body took over and she remembered how to breathe, how to put herself into the song and carry each tone to fullness. Mr. Jameson was solid beside her, his singing voice even fuller than she had imagined. When her pitch wavered, he was there, and soon their voices began to blend in a most pleasing manner. Unbidden, her eyes met his, and the appreciation there nearly made her lose the words. She forced her concentration back to the final phrases of the song.

Samantha was giggling as she played a last flourish on the piano.

"Splendid!" Mr. Jameson said. "Miss Waverly, you have a deft touch on the keyboard. And Viscountess—your voice is lovely."

Diana smiled back at him. The parlor had not rung with such happy sounds for too long. It seemed that Mr. Jameson would be a splendid substitute.

The clock on the mantel struck the hour, and Samantha let out a protest. "So soon? But we've just begun!"

Indeed, the time had sped. "Thank you, Mr. Jameson. Shall we expect you next week?"

"I would be delighted." He took Diana's hand and, bowing, lifted it to his lips.

The warm press of his mouth on her skin sent a shock of

sensation through her. It was very forward, yet she could not bring herself to reprove him, not with the heat of his kiss disordering her senses.

Still clasping her hand, he looked into her eyes—a look full of promise that made her heart race. "Until next Wednesday."

***

The tea shop on Bond Street was filled with the cheerful babble of conversation. Diana had requested a table in the nook—the safest place for a chat with Lucy, whose voice had a tendency to carry.

"Tell me, darling." Lucy arched an elegant eyebrow. "Is Mr. Jameson proving to be… satisfactory? I'd like to know if my recommendation was well-advised."

Mr. Jameson. Diana let out a slow breath.

She could not stop thinking of him—his grey eyes and handsome features, the confidence that accompanied his every movement. The past three Wednesdays had found her with a giddy lightness of spirit. She was attuned to each nuance of his expression, addicted to the heat that his slow smiles sent through her. At the conclusion of every session, he had kissed her hand. Last Wednesday, his lips had seemed to linger, the heat of his breath playing against her skin for a long moment. The memory of it sent a fluttery breathlessness winging through her even now.

"He…." Diana ran her fingertip back and forth across the rim of her cup. "He seems an excellent teacher—very patient with Samantha, and kind. She is enjoying music lessons far more than she ever has before. It's a pity he's only a *temporary* tutor. There's a certain quality about him…"

She took a hasty swallow of tea. Goodness, she shouldn't be prattling on. Whatever secret thoughts she had of the new piano tutor should stay exactly that—secret. Although, of anyone, Lucy would understand.

Her friend tilted her head, a speculative light in her eyes. "Why Diana. Are you developing an *interest* in Mr. Jameson? How marvelous. As I told you, I think he would prove an excellent diversion. You should commence an affair immediately."

Diana set her cup down so quickly that a bit of tea sloshed over the edge. "Lucy you are shocking."

Even worse than Lucy's suggestions were the images that flooded Diana's mind. Heat bloomed in her cheeks. What if Mr. Jameson did not stop when he kissed her hand? What if he continued, his warm lips laying kisses up her arm, along her neck? What if he reached her mouth and covered it with his own?

Her friend gave her a shrewd look. "High time you began thinking of yourself. You're out of formal mourning now. And you've admitted that your marriage to Lord Waverly was never one of deep passion."

"A marriage does not need passion if it has respect and…" She searched for the proper word. "Goodwill."

Lucy waved her hand. "Goodwill is all very well, in its place. But now you have an opportunity—you should seize it! If you are careful and discreet, no-one will suspect. You are free to follow your heart, or your whims—or both."

Lucy made it sound so simple.

"I must admit…" Her chest tightened, excitement firing through her blood as she spoke aloud the words she had been holding inside for weeks. "I find Mr. Jameson quite attractive. And his manner very pleasing."

Lucy nodded approval. "Indeed."

"What does it mean," Diana continued, "when a man's presence makes one feel so very *awake*? I can scarcely sleep for thoughts of him, and when I do, my dreams are...." She lowered her voice. "Oh, my dreams are most wicked."

"That is excellent news." Lucy's eyes were bright. "Perhaps you should make them come true."

Diana dropped her gaze to the tablecloth. "I doubt I'm ready to embark on such a course." It was one thing to indulge in such imaginations, quite another to act upon them. She had never considered herself bold of spirit.

"Well." Lucy dabbed her lips with her napkin. "It is your choice—but regardless, it's high time you began going out in society again. Gracious, Diana, people will scarcely remember you if you keep yourself locked away."

"In due time, Lucy." Her friend was a master at maneuvering people when she thought she knew what was best for them. Which was most of the time. "There's Samantha to think of, and—well, I'm comfortable as I am." Though she was markedly less content since a certain piano tutor had come into her well-ordered life.

"Comfortable?" Lucy lifted her nose in disdain. "That's almost as bad as *goodwill*. You need more interesting words to fill your life. *Passion*, for one. And *delight*. And best of all," her eyes sparked with mischief, "best of all—*ravishment*."

"Lucy!" Diana clapped a hand to her mouth to stifle her giggles. "You're outrageous!"

Her friend joined her laughter, oblivious to the disapproving looks of the nearby patrons. When their mirth finally subsided, Lucy assumed the commanding tones of Lady Pembroke.

"Call me what you please," she said. "I only speak the truth. Regardless of your obvious fascination with the new piano tutor, you *will* come to the musicale I'm hosting on Tuesday. It will be a small gathering—nothing too overwhelming. I'll expect you promptly at eight."

"I—"

"Pray, do not disappoint me. If you don't arrive promptly, I'll dispatch my burliest footmen to fetch you."

"Oh very well," Diana said. There was no arguing with Lucy. "As long as there is no more talk of affairs and…." She could not even say the word *ravishment* aloud, though it echoed through her thoughts. "I'll come to your musicale." She made no promises, however, as to how late she would stay.

Her friend gave a nod of satisfaction, then consulted her dainty silver pocket-watch, as if recalling something urgent. "Goodness, the time has flown! I'm nearly late for the modiste. Delightful to see you, Diana. Til Tuesday." She brushed a kiss across Diana's cheek, then hurried off, leaving Diana alone with her unsettled thoughts.

Their chat had left an edgy restlessness humming through her. Her carriage awaited outside, the driver ready to take her wherever she pleased. If only she knew where that might be.

Diana gathered her reticule and pelisse and left the shop. The air outside was pleasantly warm, and she turned her face up to the pale May sun. It was too lovely a day to waste in simply going back to Waverly House and going over menus with the cook.

She lingered, looking in the shop windows. A glorious

fan painted with swans—she could nearly imagine herself with it at some ball, laughing and dancing. Or that bracelet set with sapphires, clasped about her wrist. It was frivolous, the gems sparkling beautifully in their settings. Still, she turned away from the window. No purchase could soothe her restiveness.

She had just resolved to return home when she caught sight of a certain broad-shouldered, brown-haired gentleman striding toward her. Sparks raced through her entire body. Mr. Jameson! The loveliness of the day exploded into fiery brilliance.

He met her eyes, a smile spreading across his face as he made his way to her side.

"Viscountess." He doffed his top hat. "It's a fine day. Would you care to join me for a stroll in St. James's Park?"

"That would be," —ill-advised, besotted as she had become with him—"...delightful."

He offered his arm and she tucked her hand through with no hesitation. She was keenly aware of the places their bodies touched, and it was difficult to resist the urge to lean too close.

They walked side-by-side down Bond Street to the park. The feel of his firmly muscled forearm was not disguised even through the layers of his coat and her glove, and she found it deliciously distracting. The rest of him seemed as toned and muscular as his arm. Diana shot him a sideways glance. His well-fitted breeches showed his thighs flexing taut with every step, and his stomach seemed perfectly flat beneath the blue silk of his waistcoat. Lucy's words echoed through her. *Passion. Delight.*

The green trees of St. James's closed over them as they entered the long promenade. A lazy pond curved to one side, insects buzzing beside the water. The day was fine, the scene peaceful, but Diana felt unbalanced and strangely giddy.

There were so many questions she dare not ask. They scalded her tongue. She wanted to know everything about him, yet was afraid the answers would spoil the perfection of the day. Where are you from? Have you a wife? A mistress? She swallowed them unspoken.

"Do you enjoy teaching the piano?" she finally asked.

He nodded, his twilight eyes regarding her. "I'm finding a great deal of satisfaction in it. Miss Samantha is a quick study, and a fine musician. As are you, my lady. Have you ever considered taking lessons on the piano?"

"Taking lessons myself?" She blinked up at him. "I have always simply sung, Mr. Jameson. That is enough for me."

"How do you know?" His hand covered hers. "You should try something new. You might find that you like it very well." His smile held more than a little wickedness. Goodness! Was he suggesting…

Diana dropped her gaze, hoping her blush was hidden by the fashionable plumes in her bonnet. It seemed to be an afternoon for improper conversations.

With a sudden daring, she asked, "If I were to become your pupil, when might these tutorials occur? Before or after Samantha's lessons?"

"Not on Wednesday." His voice was warm honey, drizzling over her senses. "My instruction would require sufficient uninterrupted time. Perhaps Thursdays."

"Surely your other pupils would object to the change of schedule."

The pressure of his hand over hers increased. "It's all a matter of priority."

They were passing a weeping willow, the leaves tender and newly green, swaying lightly in the breeze. Diana took a deep breath of the soft air to steady herself.

"I would be your priority on Thursdays?"

He stopped and gave her an intent look. "You would be my priority every day."

Oh, it was the purest flirtation, she knew it, but still her heartbeat stumbled in giddy joy.

"Really, Mr. Jameson—"

"Call me Nicholas." He drew her off the pathway, beneath the sheltering canopy of the willow tree.

"Nicholas." She half-whispered it, a bold exhilaration tingling through her. "Then you must call me Diana."

Suddenly they were not tutor and lady any longer, but only man and woman. The air between them was alive with possibility, the spaces where bodies were, and were not. And could be.

Had she had taken complete leave of her senses? She did not care. In one twist of an afternoon a gate had opened that she had thought closed forever. A pathway back to herself. Not the young widow. Not the capable stepmother, but *her*, Diana, who had once been full of passionate dreams.

Her senses were sharpened by an almost unbearable anticipation. Everything was magnified—the light breeze, the scent of his bergamot cologne, the sound of water quietly lapping the shore. There was something excruciatingly wonderful about knowing she was about to be kissed. He leaned forward, a smile dancing in his eyes, and she tilted her face up to him.

His mouth brushed hers, their lips meeting, parting, meeting again—like a musician sounding a note, over and over, until it was perfect. She slid her hands up to his shoulders, learning the shape of his mouth against hers.

He increased the pressure of his lips. The smooth slide of his tongue against her lower lip made sparks scatter through her, and she willingly opened her mouth to him. Nicholas dipped his tongue inside. He tasted of tea and desire, and something inside her gave way, melting like late frost before the sun.

This was no debutante's kiss. It carried the full knowledge of how a man and a woman fit together. The plunge of his tongue into her mouth, her yielding softness— all this was part of the dance, a promise of deeper intimacies. She pressed herself closer to him, yearning spiraling out from her center.

Nicholas Jameson was a wonderful kisser.

It was more than the way he fitted his lips so perfectly over hers, or the velvety warmth of his tongue. More than the feel of his hand curving around her shoulder, the brush of his thumb over her bare collarbone. His kiss flared through her entire body.

She was aware of her toes, warm and content in her buttoned boots. Her legs, cased in silk stockings with ribbon garters above her knees. The soft cotton of her chemise where it lay against her skin. The fine silk of her drawers, heated at the juncture of her legs.

And she was aware of him. Wonderfully aware of the slight roughness of his jaw as he kissed her, the warm maleness of him as they leaned into one another, the smell of spring willows and fine wool, and arousal. His. Hers.

They kissed and kissed, and then it was over. Diana opened her eyes and smiled up at him, as though she had just woken from a perfect dream.

***

Diana set a smile across her face and nodded at the conversation flowing past. Oh, she should never have agreed to come to Lucy's musicale. She had no heart for it. It had been too long—she did not know any of the current *on dits* and was relegated to standing awkwardly at the edges of the company.

Besides, how could she possibly be a witty conversationalist when all she could think of was Nicholas's hands at her waist, drawing her into that intoxicating kiss?

With his talk of "piano lessons" had he truly been suggesting that they become lovers? Her pulse sped at the thought. Her sleep had been restless, her skin too sensitive ever since that kiss. Even now the slide of her petticoats against her legs sent a shiver through her. What if Nicholas touched her there—and everywhere? How would it feel to embrace without the constraints of coat and skirts, to lay together skin-to-skin? Her throat went dry with longing at the thought.

"Ladies and Gentlemen!" Lucy stood at the front of the room and clapped her hands together. "Please take your seats so the musicale may commence."

Diana sidled to the end of the back row. Perhaps, once they put out the lights, she could make her escape. She did not think she could bear more awkward conversation during the intermission.

The featured performer of the evening was introduced—a young harpist who was the newest musical sensation. The room darkened, and Diana let out a breath of relief. Now she could lose herself in thoughts of Nicholas. She closed her eyes as the harpist plucked the first chord.

Someone took the seat next to her, startling her from her reverie. Cloth rustled, and then the familiar scent of bergamot cologne tickled her nose. Her eyes flew open and she turned, surprise jolting through her as she glimpsed the white gleam of Nicholas's grin. It was as if her thoughts had summoned him here.

He leaned close. "Good evening, Diana." His breath was warm against her cheek.

"Nicholas—whatever are you doing here?"

His hand found hers in the dark, his clasp sure as he twined his naked fingers through her gloved ones. The intimacy of it made her gasp. Surely her heart was beating so loudly that everyone could hear.

"Come," he said.

A glissando of harp notes shivered through her. What were his plans for her? What if he had no plans?

She would never know unless she went with him into the wicked shadows. For a moment fear held her in her seat. She could not, she could not.... Then he tugged gently at her hand and desire rose up in a wave and lifted her to her feet.

Nicholas drew her out of the darkened drawing room. The lamps in the hallway shed a beckoning light, their flames echoing the excitement flickering through her. No-one was there to mark their illicit departure. He led her down the hall and up a short flight of stairs, the music growing fainter behind them. Without pause, he opened a door and ushered her through.

They were in the library. Lamplight glinted on gold-lettered spines and she breathed in the scent of books and leather. And Nicholas. He closed the door, shutting out the last lilting notes. When he turned back to her his expression was intent, his grey eyes lit with desire. For her.

Diana caught her breath, heat blossoming inside her.

Without a word, he strode forward and took her in his arms. Her breasts pressed against his silver-embroidered waistcoat—softness against hardness, woman against man. Her breath swept between her lips, flavored with passion. When he bent his head, she eagerly opened her mouth.

It was as delicious as she had remembered. His tongue played against hers, sweet and hot, and she felt her fears dissolve into acceptance. A low, insistent pulse began within her, as if she were an instrument responding to his touch.

She slid her hands to his shoulders, then dropped them in frustration to tug urgently at the fingertips of her gloves. She needed to feel his bare skin beneath her palms, the planes of his cheek and jaw, the softness of his dark hair tangled between her fingers.

He helped her strip the gloves off, as hungry as she. For a moment he held them dangling in his hand and gave her a penetrating look.

She stepped forward and kissed him. By heaven, she had made her choice, and she was going to embrace it with all the long-banked fire in her soul. She tasted his laughter, and then his arms came around her and the kiss deepened.

So sweet and fierce. Embers flickered to flame, scorched to need. His palms smoothed the emerald satin of her gown and she leaned into his touch. There was no doubt he found her desirable—his body proved it, the hardness of him pressing against her center. He bunched her skirts in his hands drew them up, cool air caressing her legs.

Wordlessly, she stepped back and let him pull her gown off. Her chemise tangled in her arms, and then it, too was gone. She stood before him, naked but for her undergarments. It was outrageous, and wonderful.

"So beautiful," he said, his eyes alight with hunger.

He stroked his hands up her sides, then covered her breasts. She sucked in a sharp breath. Little fires quivered beneath his palms, and she could feel her nipples tauten under his touch. She arched into his hands, threw her head back, and sighed. What a picture she must make, wearing only her stockings and drawers, wanton and sensual under the hands of this darkly handsome gentleman.

But he was wearing too much clothing. Her hands went to his cravat, making quick work of the elegant knot. Next, the buttons of his waistcoat, his fine linen shirt. She tugged the fabric free of his breeches and, hands trembling, pushed his shirt open. His chest was firmly muscled, a light dusting of hair tickling her fingertips as she stroked his skin.

He made a sound of longing, then pulled her to him, his chest hot and hard against hers. It was as delicious as she had imagined. Another blazing kiss, and then he stepped back. She helped him pull off his coat and shirt, then he scraped his boots off and removed his breeches.

Diana peeked between her lashes, curious and eager, then caught her breath at the sight of him. He was erect and strong, and she felt suddenly powerful, to bring him to such a rampant state.

Henry had always insisted on taking his husbandly prerogatives with the lights off, the two of them securely between the sheets. He had never made her feel like this, had never openly admired her, or told her she was beautiful. It had been pleasant enough, their marital relations, but nothing like the fire that now seared through her.

And that fire was nothing compared to the sensation that engulfed her when Nicholas took her in his arms and dipped his hand between her legs. This tempest of want scorching her to her soul—this was new. This was *passion*.

"Ah!" she cried as his fingers stroked and played beneath her drawers. She gripped the strong sinews of his arms—she was going to fly to bits if she did not hold tightly to him.

Nicholas withdrew his hand and she moaned in protest. With a devilish smile, he stripped off her drawers, then maneuvered her backward until her legs bumped the settee. They tumbled down together onto the gold velvet cushions and he braced himself over her, setting his member where his fingers had been. Slowly, inexorably, he pressed forward, opening her. Their gazes locked as their bodies fitted together, imperfectly at first. Then easier as he slid back, and forward again.

"Yes," she breathed.

It was lovely and heated and, oh, she couldn't bear how deliberately Nicholas moved in her. She caught at his shoulders and tilted her hips up, urging him to stroke deeper, faster. His breath hitched as he quickened his pace, the pulse at the side of his neck beating urgently.

More. Yes, and *more*, until the pressure she felt coiling inside her finally released, exploded like an errant firework to spangle her senses with light and color.

He let out a muffled shout and pulled free, spilling himself on the fine linen of his shirt. Sweat gleamed on his arms, his chest.

She let out a sigh of pleasure, her body sated, her whole being utterly, perfectly content. She brushed her fingers through his silky hair. Nicholas Jameson—masterful and tender, patient and passionate. The door to her heart swung open.

A smile illuminated his face and he brought one hand up to cup her cheek. "Now that, my Diana, was splendid indeed."

***

It was Wednesday.

Diana sat in the music room, waiting for the sound of the knocker to reverberate through the entry. Nicholas would be here at any moment. Anticipation fluttered all the way down to her toes.

Samantha played another run of notes, then glanced at the clock. "Perhaps Mr. Jameson has forgotten," she said. "He has not developed the habit of coming to Waverly House."

"Nonsense. He's been our piano tutor for weeks now." Diana infused her voice with certainty. "He has only been delayed twenty minutes. There could be any number of reasons for it."

"Perhaps he has been crushed by a carriage, or—"

"Samantha, enough! I'm certain Mr. Jameson will be here momentarily."

After the lesson, she would ask him to stay for tea. She would ask him everything, and have no fear of the answers.

He had brought music and light into Waverly House. He had coaxed her from behind her comfortable boundaries and shown her what true passion was. Every day from now on would be richer because of it. She would be richer. The memory of his touches, his words, flared through her. She had never felt so beautiful.

"It's half past the hour." Samantha sounded glum. "He's not coming."

Diana bit her lip. Where was he? Anticipation curdled into apprehension. "Practice a bit more, dear. I'll go check with the butler." Though of course he would have shown Mr. Jameson straight in.

The heels of her boots clicked across the marble floor of the entryway. When she pulled the heavy front door open, the butler raised his eyebrows, but said nothing.

The street outside was quiet. No handsome grey-eyed man striding up to her door, no cabs to be seen the entire length of the block. She stood on the threshold for several minutes, the distant clamor of London washing past her, but the street remained empty.

The butler cleared his throat, and she slowly shut the door. Head high, she re-entered the parlor.

Samantha's expression lit. "Is he...?"

"No. Not yet." She couldn't help but glance at the clock. The entire hour had run. Did she mean nothing to him? An ugly sob rose in her throat.

"Mama?" Samantha sent her a concerned glance.

Diana swallowed. "I suppose something important has detained him. You may go." She blinked rapidly against the sting of tears.

Samantha gave her a hug, then slipped out of the room. Diana bowed her head. Had she been such a fool to listen to Lucy? It had not felt that way at the time. But it seemed she had made a dreadful mistake.

She had practically seduced him. The piano tutor. He must be too embarrassed to face her, here with her stepdaughter, after what had been between them. He must despise her, think her a woman of exceedingly loose morals, to take such base liberties with her employee.

Yet he was far more to her than that. Her heart ached with lost possibilities.

They had, neither of them, promised more than a single hour of unbridled desire. Their banter about tutoring had hardly been talk of courtship, of love. If her actions had been spurred by deeper feelings, as she must now admit, what had she been to him? Only a willing female—one whom he evidently had no more use for.

She knew nothing about him. Nothing except that he made her feel more alive, more daring, than anyone she had ever met. And now it was ended.

She could not bear the thought.

***

The servants at Lucy's mansion knew Diana well enough to admit her without hesitation.

"Is Lady Pembroke in?" she asked.

"She is, madam," Lucy's butler said. "She is taking the air in the garden. Shall I escort you?"

"That won't be necessary." If, as she feared, she was going to burst into tears the moment she saw her friend, she would prefer to do so unobserved.

"As you wish." The butler bowed her toward the French doors overlooking Lucy's grounds.

Diana stepped out and took a deep breath of the late-spring air. Lucy would know what to do. A woman of her experience surely knew all about broken hearts.

Rounding the yew hedge, Diana heard voices. Lucy's. And a man's, painfully familiar. Sudden fear knifing through her, she crept forward.

"Damn it Lucy, I have to tell her." Nicholas's voice was strained. "It's gone too far. She deserves to know the truth."

"She's not ready." Lucy sounded resolute. "Think up some excuse—tell her you were unavoidably detained. But don't tell her what you and I have been up to."

Ice swept over Diana, comprehension settling cold and dreadful against her bones. Lucy's talk of handsome piano tutors. Nicholas, here in her garden, using Lucy's given name so intimately. His presence at the musicale last night, his familiarity with Lucy's house....

Anger flared through her. The scoundrel! To use her so, when all along he had been Lucy's lover. What a contemptible rake, to seduce Diana—here of all places.

She swept out from behind the hedge. "Unavoidably detained?" She raked her gaze over Nicholas. His eyes widened and he took a step toward her.

Lucy grabbed at his arm. "Diana. We were just speaking of you—"

"Yes," she said. The word was coated in frost. "And what exactly were the two of you doing while my *employee* was supposed to be giving a piano lesson?"

Nicholas shook himself free of Lucy's grasp. "Let me explain—"

"You should have explained before the musicale." Her voice caught, snagged on memory. "But it seemed you had *other* priorities. Perhaps you had forgotten you had a music lesson to teach while you were 'unavoidably detained.' You've behaved most unprofessionally, sir."

She fought to speak against the tightness in her throat. Nicholas reached for her and she pulled away. "I no longer need your services, Mr. Jameson. You are *fired*."

Hot tears blurring her vision, she turned and ran. Dimly she heard Nicholas calling after her, Lucy remonstrating, but she did not pause. She rushed back to her carriage and flung herself inside, slamming the door before the footman could even approach.

It was far worse than she had suspected. And still a part of her had wanted to stay, to listen to his pleas. She was so unbearably weak. As the wheels rattled over the cobblestones, she dropped her head into her hands and abandoned herself to grief.

***

"Mama?" Samantha pushed open the parlor door. "Are you ill? I had cook make you some chocolate."

She entered the room, carefully balancing a tray holding the silver chocolate pot and two cups. Diana mustered a smile for her stepdaughter and hoped her eyes were not too red from weeping.

"Thank you, dear. I am not unwell, just a bit tired." Did heartsickness count as an illness? She did not think so. "Come, sit by me." She patted the settee.

Samantha set the tray down and curled up close. Diana put her arm around the girl's shoulders and gave them a squeeze—the reassurance as much for herself as for her stepdaughter.

"I have some unhappy news for you." She heaved a breath. "Mr. Jameson will not be returning as your piano tutor."

"Oh." The girl's shoulders slumped. "That is too bad. He was ever so charming—and smelled much better than Mr. Bent."

Diana smiled—it was the only way to keep the tears from welling up again. "That he did." She leaned over and rested her head against Samantha's. All brightness was not gone from her life, no matter how dreary the day might feel.

"My lady." The butler bowed at the parlor door. "Forgive me for interrupting. You have a caller. Are you at home?"

She straightened. Nicholas wouldn't dare—not if he had a shred of sense. It had to be Lucy. One way or another, she would have to face her friend.

"Yes, I am receiving."

"Very good." He extended the silver salver, a vellum card centered on it. "Shall I show him in?"

"Him?" Her lips pressed tightly together she took the card. If it were Mr. Jameson.... "The Marquess of Somerton?" She stared at the unfamiliar name. "I don't believe I know any such person. Please tell the gentleman I am not taking visitors today." Particularly uninvited ones. She could not face another stranger in her house.

"Very good." The butler departed.

"Thank you for the chocolate, Samantha." Diana gave her stepdaughter another quick embrace. Really, she ought to bestir herself. There was no use sitting in the parlor when it held such memories of Nicholas.

"I'm glad it helped. Chocolate often does." The girl jumped up and gathered the cups and tray, then paused and kissed Diana's cheek before bustling out the door.

Voices filtered from the hallway, and then the butler was back.

"I am sorry, my lady, but the marquess insists he will see you. He vowed to toss me into the street if I stood in his way."

Diana rose, then nearly folded back down on the settee when she saw who had followed the butler in.

Nicholas. The breath squeezed from her lungs while a wild, giddy clamor started up in her blood.

"Please go," she breathed. No matter how much she wanted to remain unmoved, the expression in his familiar grey eyes nearly undid her.

He was carrying an exuberant bouquet of roses, which he handed to the butler. "See to these."

Clever man—if he had given her the flowers, she would have flung them back in his face. As soon as the butler departed, she turned on Nicholas. Piano tutor, marquess—whomever he claimed to be today.

"How dare you?" Her ribs felt as though a band of silk were wrapped around them, pulled too tight. "To think, what we did under Lucy's very roof! And then you come here, bullying my servants, and—"

"Diana." He closed the distance between them and took her by the shoulders. Fool that she was, she could not move away from his touch. "I don't think my cousin begrudges the use of her library. She has done far worse in my best carriage, with never a word of apology."

"Your... your cousin?" She blinked up at him, her heart catching with a wild, irrational hope. "Lady Pembroke is your cousin?"

"Yes." A mischievous light sparked in his eyes. "Lucy. My meddling plague of a cousin. The one who bribed Mr. Bent to take an extended holiday, then suggested I pose as a piano tutor and tempt you out of hiding." He shook his head. "But it didn't work."

"No?" She had been tempted, all too easily. Even now she felt breathless.

He smiled at her—rueful and amused all at once. "My plan was to slowly draw you out. To, as Lucy put it, 'help ease you from your widowhood.' But falling in love with you made things bloody awkward."

Falling in love? Happy tears tingled at the back of her eyes. The Marquess of Somerton? "But...you make an excellent piano tutor."

His hands tightened on her shoulders and he drew her forward. "I assure you, I make a far better suitor."

She went willingly, lifting her face to his kiss. A kiss that swirled her senses, even as it anchored her fully to herself. A kiss full of passion. Delight. Life.

~THE END~

To Wed the Earl

Miss Miranda Price pressed the latch of the French doors leading into Edgerton Manor's library. The metal was wet with dew, and clammy against her chilled fingers. Behind her, the moonlit garden rustled, alive with night creatures and the danger of discovery. Heart beating loud in her throat, she pulled the door open.

Warm air washed over her, filled with the comforting, musty smell of books. She stepped inside and closed the door with a quiet click. It was dark in the library – darker than the garden outside. Thank goodness she'd had the foresight to tuck a candle stub into her skirt pocket.

Moving through the room by memory, Miranda avoided the edges of a long table and fetched up before the hearth. With cautious fingers, she searched for the tinderbox on the mantel. Her fingertips brushed the curve of an ormolu clock and the base of a small globe, then landed on the rounded shape of the tinderbox.

It took several tries, but at last she managed to light her candle. The warm flame made the shadows gather more thickly in the corners of the room. She swallowed, throat tight with apprehension. *Stay calm. No need to worry.*

She would find her journal and slip out again, none the wiser. In another half-hour she would be safely home at Wyckerly and tucked beneath her covers, with her book once again hidden under the mattress.

What a fool she'd been, to leave it in the study! With its leather binding, it did look similar to the tomes her father, Viscount Wyckerly, regularly borrowed from Edgerton Manor. She supposed she couldn't blame the housekeeper for gathering up her journal along with the rest. Still, it had given her several moments of panic when she'd discovered her book was gone.

It was here, though, in the Edgerton's library. It must be.

Miranda lifted her candle, the flame flickering, and scanned the room for a stack of unshelved books. There – on the table by the door. She hurried over, the tight band of worry about her ribs easing when she spotted the scrolled gilt pattern on the spine of her journal.

One-handed, she pulled it from the stack. The books on top teetered, and horror washed over her. She blew the candle-stub out, then lunged to catch them. Too late. The thud of books hitting the floor echoed like cannon fire through the quiet manor.

Miranda froze, barely breathing, but no anxious cries came from the hallway. No servants burst into the room to investigate. Perhaps she was safe. She waited another few moments, then carefully felt about the floor, picking up and restacking the books.

Holding her journal close, she turned and moved back toward the French doors.

A draft stirred the air at the back of her neck. Then, from nowhere, a hand grasped her arm.

Miranda shrieked and tried to pull away.

"Be quiet, you fool," a voice said. "Or do you want to be discovered?"

Oh no. Those low, male tones were all too familiar. She

had been caught – and by none other than Edward Havens, the Earl of Edgerton himself. Her fingers tightened around her journal.

"It would appear I already have been discovered." She forced her voice into a semblance of calm, though her nerves careened with alarm. "Release me."

"I don't think so." His tone held a spark of amusement, a glint of gold in a dark stream. "I'd like to see who is breaking into my library well past midnight."

"You weren't expected home until tomorrow," she said.

"What a well-informed thief you are, to recognize me so handily." His hand slid down her arm and encircled her wrist. "Come here, so I may return the favor."

He walked to the doors, pulling her along with him. She had no chance to wrench free from his firm grip. And even if she gained her freedom, where would she run? He would catch up with her in an instant. Miranda bit her lip.

She would simply explain, he would let her go, and that would be the end of it.

Moonlight spilled through the glass panes. The earl towed her directly into the light, then tilted his head and inspected her. His backlit form was a looming shadow against the silver night.

"Ah," he said. "Miss Miranda Price. Still a creature of mischief, I see."

Heat rushed into her cheeks and she yanked her wrist out of his grasp. Once again, she was reminded of how much she disliked the man.

"Now that you see I am not some thief sneaking in to steal your family fortune," she said, "I shall bid you goodnight."

She pulled her cloak about her, keeping the book tucked safely beneath her arm, and reached for the latch.

"Not yet." He took her by the shoulders. "What are you hiding under your cloak?"

His warm breath fanned across her cheek, spiced with the faint scent of brandy. Heavens, he was annoyingly close.

"Nothing that concerns you." Her heart hammered in her chest.

"Miss Price – you are removing a book from my library. I think it *does* concern me."

She swallowed. "It's mine. It was mistakenly delivered here earlier today. I merely came to retrieve it."

"In the middle of the night? Let me see the book."

Her breath caught. She couldn't show him her journal! Among other things, it was full of scathing condemnations of him.

"I assure you – "

"No need for assurances." Faster than she'd thought possible, he flipped her cloak back and snatched the book. "I'll verify it for myself."

"Sir!" She reached for her precious journal, but he spun away and strode back into the darkened room.

As she followed him, her skirts caught on the corner of the table. In the time it took for her to regain her balance and catch up, he had deftly lit the sconce atop the mantel.

"Give my book back," she said, holding out her hand.

"One moment." In the light of the candle, he opened the tooled leather cover.

"The journal belongs to me," she said, trying to keep the edge of desperation from her voice. Edward Havens could *not* read her journal. "I demand you return it immediately."

One eyebrow rose and he shook his head, the light gleaming on strands of pure gold in his tawny hair. He shot her a glance from eyes so dark blue they seemed almost black.

"I'm captivated by your character descriptions, Miss Price. I had no idea you aspired to be a novelist. Hateful Havens – the man sounds quite the villain."

Mortification rushed through her, a wave of heat rising from her toes to the crown of her head.

"I was but a child when I began keeping this journal. You must forgive my youthful fancies."

This was dreadful – her worst nightmare. Edward Havens reading her journal, and mocking it in her presence. It was the very thing she had stolen over here to prevent. Such bitter irony that her actions had made this horror come to pass. She folded her arms tightly over her churning stomach.

He flipped to the front page, a smile twisting his lips.

"I see. Yes, five years ago was certainly a lifetime. No doubt you've become much wiser since attaining the ripe age of twenty." He glanced down at the page again. "I see here that I am a scoundrel and a rake. Do you have a wide acquaintance with the type? West Dorset is reputed to be rife with such villains."

"I've heard the stories about you." Heavens – how prim she sounded.

But it was true. Ever since his father's death a year ago, the new Earl of Edgerton had descended into debauchery and scandal. He was often mentioned in the London gossip rags – not that she would admit to poring over them looking for his name. No, she was most concerned for her brother's reputation.

"Stories from your brother, I suspect." He closed the

journal and thrust it toward her. "I wouldn't believe everything Charlie tells you. It appears that a talent for fiction runs in your family."

She snatched the book from him and tucked it beneath her arm. "You are a terrible influence on him."

"No doubt." His tone was dry.

There was no use arguing with the man, not here in his own library. She had sent letters to Charlie, begging him to cease his acquaintance with Edward Havens, but her brother had refused to cut his old friend.

"Well then. Welcome home, my lord." She bobbed him a shallow curtsey. "I bid you goodnight."

She would not dwell upon the shame scorching her. The worst had happened – the earl now knew precisely what she thought of him. At least she had good company. Everyone else in Dorset was well aware of his wickedness. Except, perhaps, his mother.

Miranda turned toward the French doors and gathered her cloak more tightly about her.

"Wait." He set his hand on her arm. "Did you come here alone?"

Her heart stilled, like a hare suddenly in the hunter's sights. Even she, plain Miranda Price, knew better than to admit to a man with his reputation that she was unescorted.

"I…" She forced out a light laugh. "Of course not. My maid is waiting outside. In the rose arbor."

"I will take you to her, and see you both on your way."

"No need." She pushed open the door and stepped into the moonlit garden.

The earl was right behind her.

"Miss Price, I cannot let you wander alone about my

estate in the middle of the night. The rose arbor, you say?"

He took her elbow in a firm grip and steered her down a path lined with color-leached flowers. At the end stood the solid, arching shadow of the arbor. The dark vines were spangled with blossoms, pink by day, now silver in the moonlight. Miranda swallowed and slowed her steps, but they arrived all too soon.

"Empty," he said. "It seems your maid has abandoned you. Not the most reliable of servants. I will have to see you home, myself."

There was something in his voice, a barely perceptible amusement that told her he suspected she had come by herself.

"I shall have words with her," Miranda said. "But in any case, it is late. I can make my way home without misfortune. No doubt you crave the comfort of your bed."

The moment the word was out of her mouth, she wished she could call it back. Heat flamed in her cheeks. Proper young ladies did not mention beds – especially not to scoundrelly earls. Especially not when alone with them, in their gardens, at night.

"You are kindness itself," he said. "My bed, however, is not particularly comforting. Seeing as how it is empty."

She stared at him, aware that her mouth was open in a soundless inhalation.

"Forgive me, Miss Price. I know you are a young lady of sheltered sensibilities." The amusement in his tone became more pronounced. "Of course, I was not suggesting you join me beneath the covers."

Her heart stuttered at the thought. That he would even say such a thing to her was shocking.

Any doubts she had harbored about his reputation being exaggerated quickly evaporated. Certainly, the papers loved to speculate over his exploits. The Earl of Edgerton was rumored to be irresistible to opera dancers, widows, the wives of visiting dignitaries. Indeed, she had lost count of his supposed dalliances.

And here she was, in the moonlit rose-garden with him. Once, it would have made her giddy with joy. She would have stared at his handsome features, delighted in the sheen of starlight over his hair, dreamed of being wrapped in his arms while he kissed her senseless.

She stepped away from him and summoned her frostiest demeanor.

"You, sir, are reprehensible. I'm surprised you feel the need to escort me home."

His mouth twisted. In the pale light it was impossible to tell if it was a wry smile, or something more bitter.

"Despite your beliefs, I am not devoid of all honor. I presume the path to Wyckerly is still clear?"

He gestured to the half-wild woods that lay beyond the formal garden. Although it was a good five miles between their estates by road, the secret path cut the distance to a quarter of that length.

"Clear enough," she said, though her cloak and hem were damp from brushing against overhanging bushes on the walk to Edgerton Manor.

She lifted her chin and hurried to the border of the woods. If he wanted to follow, she could not stop him – but she would not endeavor to be pleasant to the man. Especially as he found it so amusing to mock her 'sheltered sensibilities.'

They walked in silence, broken only by the rustling of

creatures in the underbrush and the distant hooting of an owl. At the half-way point – a small clearing marked with a fallen log – he cleared his throat.

"Are you still pursuing your study of geometry?" he asked.

"Yes." He was not entitled to know more.

"It seems you're no stranger to my library." There was a hint of accusation in his voice.

"Your mother has kindly offered use of it to both my father and myself."

"Even at midnight?"

She squeezed the book under her arm. "I told you. My journal was mistakenly returned along with the books that belong in your library."

"And you couldn't wait until a more acceptable time to reclaim it?"

"I didn't want…" She squirmed inside at the thought of the few pages he had read. High time to change the subject. "Speaking of the late hour, is my brother now home as well? Weren't the two of you traveling together?"

"Yes – my coachman brought Charlie home as soon as I disembarked at the hall. No doubt he's sleeping soundly. It was a long journey from London." He let out a weary, somewhat theatrical sigh.

"It's not my fault you insisted on following me about the woods, when you could be… resting." She would not say the word *bed* again.

Ahead, the lights of Wyckerly shone through the thinning trees. She hurried forward, then paused at the edge of the lawn.

"You may leave me here," she said. "It would not do for

me to be seen in your company."

"I don't think it would do for you to be seen at all – but I take your point. Goodnight, Miss Price."

She gave him a quick curtsy, then hastened across the lawn. When she reached the shelter of the side door, she glanced back. At the verge of the woods, she could just make out the glint of his fair hair where he stood, watching her.

***

Edward's mother, Lady Edgerton, rose from the striped silk divan in the sitting room and bestowed a lily-scented kiss upon his cheek. Late morning light streamed in through the windows, burnishing the polished wooden floor – and showing all too clearly the toll the former earl's death had taken on his widow.

"Welcome home, darling!"

"Hello, Mother," Edward said. "You're looking well."

It was only a slight exaggeration. A deep line scored her forehead, and her fair hair bore new strands of silver. Her face was thinner, and her eyes held a melancholy he suspected would never completely fade.

Guilt curled about his ribs like smoke – insubstantial, yet difficult to breathe through. He should not have stayed away so long. But the official mourning period was now over, and it was time, past time, to take care of his mother again.

"I had hoped to see you at breakfast." She sat again, in a rustle of primrose-yellow skirts. "Come, sit with me. You *will* be keeping country hours now that you're here? None of this lying abed until noon?"

It was not noon – it was barely ten – but he did not want

to argue the point. Edward firmed his lips and took the armchair beside his mother.

"It was a late night," he said, "but I will endeavor not to miss breakfast again."

It wasn't as if there was much of anything to do late into the evenings here in West Dorset. Except escort young ladies home through the woods. He shook his head. Charlie's younger sister had not changed one whit. She was still an oddly bookish girl – who evidently held him in great distaste. The bits of her journal he had read were florid in their descriptions of his vile character.

In any case it didn't matter. He had no intention of spending time in Miss Price's company.

"I was thinking," his mother said. "We should hold a ball. Wouldn't that be marvelous?"

A prickle of apprehension shivered up his neck. He feared his mother had only one objective in suggesting such an event.

To find him a bride.

"A ball?" he said cautiously. "I don't intend to remain at Edgerton Manor for long. A fortnight should do to sort out the finances."

"You must stay longer." There was no room for argument in her voice. "I have missed you dreadfully. Is it too much to ask for your company for a mere month?"

"Mother, you may come up to London any time you choose. There is plenty of room in the town house."

She let out a sigh. "You know the city air does not agree with me – especially in the summer. Indeed, the country is delightful this time of year. And now that I am out of mourning, we shall make it a small house party! No doubt the invitees will be pleased to depart London."

Edward crossed his arms. Though part of him wanted to dissuade her, he was relieved to see her take an interest in social gatherings once more. She had mourned her husband for over a year. It was time she rejoined Society – even if it meant he had to suffer.

"Whom do you plan to invite?" he asked.

"Well…" There was a gleam in Lady Edgerton's eyes. "The Davenports, of course – I have not seen them for some years, though Lady Davenport and I were very close in our youth. I hear their daughter Leticia has become quite a dark-haired beauty."

"Indeed."

And an avaricious one, at that. Miss Davenport had firmly set her sights on him. His friend Charlie found it amusing that, for once, Edward was the one being pursued. Edward found it far less gratifying. Especially after narrowly escaping a scene engineered by the lady that would have left him no choice but to marry her.

There was no hope his mother wouldn't invite them, considering her past friendship with Lady Davenport. He needed to take a great deal of care when dealing with Miss Davenport, or he would find himself shackled to her. *And would that be so dreadful?* an insidious voice inside him asked. At least the thing would be done, and easily enough.

"Lady Davenport and I always dreamed of our offspring making a match." His mother leaned over and patted his hand. "Not that I would dictate the direction of your heart."

"Of course not."

Only try to steer it. And it seemed Leticia Davenport had enthusiastically embraced the idea.

"We shall invite the Montforts down from London, as well," his mother said. "And the local gentry, of course. Viscount Trelling and the Prices." She tapped her fingers against her skirts. "Five eligible young ladies in all – that would make a suitable selection, don't you think?"

He mentally discounted Miranda Price, and he suspected Charlie was quite fond of Miss Trelling, though whether he would ever come up to scratch on her account was hard to say. As for the Montfort girls, both of them were barely out of the schoolroom. Which left only one eligible young lady standing – Leticia Davenport.

"I have no intention of marrying quite so soon." Might as well put it bluntly.

"Nonsense." Lady Edgerton fixed him with her bright blue eyes. "You are seven-and-twenty. It's past time for you to settle into the title. You've had a year of grace, Edward. The estate needs looking after – now *and* in the future."

The truth of it stabbed him. She was right. And though he was in no hurry to produce heirs, he had been derelict in his other duties as earl. Something had gone awry with the finances since his father's death, something his London solicitor could not explain – other than to say the problem originated here, at the estate.

So, here he was, finally ready to shoulder his responsibilities. But must he take on *all* of them at once?

"Speaking of estate business," he said, "I'm meeting with Mr. Fowler to look over the accounts today. I'm sure the matter will be cleared up promptly."

Likely something had just been overlooked, and the precipitous drop in their income would be remedied straight away.

"I'm so relieved you're home." His mother gave him a warm smile. "At dinner, you can tell me all about your adventures in London."

***

Four hours later, Edward had changed his mind. His neck ached from sitting in the hard office chair before his father's desk, going over numbers. The cramped rows of figures in Mr. Fowler's account book were beginning to blur in front of his eyes. Even the air in the room was dry and dusty, withering his brain with every breath. No solution to their sudden loss of revenues had presented itself.

"That's enough for now," Edward said, sitting up straight and rubbing his forehead. He pushed the ledger away. "Perhaps we need to go further back in the books."

"As you say, my lord." Seated across from him, Mr. Fowler closed the current ledger, his eye bright in his round face. "We can recommence this evening. I'm sure the answers are here somewhere, and with your help, I've no doubt we can find them.

"No." Edward was getting a headache from staring at those damnable numbers and trying to make sense of them. "Tomorrow afternoon is soon enough."

He needed fresh air, something to sweep the cobwebs from his head. Mathematics had never been his strong suit. He would go riding, drop in on Charlie and coax his friend to join him in a long, hard gallop. Fence-jumping seemed in order, as well.

"Very good. Tomorrow afternoon." Mr. Fowler slid the account book back into the shelves. "At least you can see that the rents have been down because of the need for improvements. The storm last winter took quite a toll on the home farm and your tenants. Extensive repairs were necessary."

"Yes, yes." Edward waved the words away like annoying gnats. "I understand the necessity."

Still, although the figures made sense, something seemed amiss. The estate was producing far less income than in the past – by hundreds of pounds. Enough that his London solicitor had become alarmed and advised Edward to look into the matter promptly.

Edward swallowed, his mouth tasting of dust. He probably should not have waited another three months before taking action – but damn it, he was not ready to be the Earl of Edgerton. He was supposed to have years ahead of him. His father had been sound in mind and body – until the day he had suddenly dropped dead in the hallway.

"Thank you, Fowler," Edward said. "I shall see you tomorrow."

"My lord." Mr. Fowler bowed, displaying the top of his balding head.

With a great deal of relief, Edward shut the study door behind him. He called for his horse and went to change into his riding jacket. If he were in London, he would pay one of his paramours a visit, but under the circumstances a different kind of ride would have to suffice.

***

"**E**dward – good morning!" Charlie Price strode into the parlor at Wyckerly, eyes sleepy and hair flattened on one side.

Edward straightened from where he lounged against the mantel. He had been idly looking at the two pen-and-ink portraits displayed above – the Price offspring in their youth. The artist had done a remarkably fine job of catching Charlie's lighthearted demeanor, and child Miranda's eyes were full of mischief. No surprise there.

"It's two in the afternoon," he said to Charlie, exasperated and amused. City or country, Charlie Price was a man who enjoyed his rest. "You lazy bones – come riding with me."

"What?" Charlie squinted out the window. "Afternoon already? Let me fetch a quick bite, and I'll join you."

"I'll wait in the gardens," Edward said.

He'd had enough of being shut inside. And it was true what his mother said – the air here was a pleasure to breathe, free of the fogs and soots of London.

"I'll meet you shortly." Charlie gave him an amiable smile and turned on his heel.

Edward shook his head. The man's idea of 'shortly' was outside the usual definition of the word. At least the gardens at Wyckerly were a pleasant place to pass the time.

He paused on the front steps, catching sight of a pale bonnet bobbing above the colorful splashes of the flowerbeds. Miss Miranda Price was strolling in the garden. Some perverse urge made him turn his direction toward her.

He brushed past a bed full of irises. Was it his imagination, or had she increased her pace away from him? She rounded the corner of a tall hedge. When Edward arrived, she was nowhere in sight. He scanned the empty gravel paths, the cheerful plantings. Where could she have gone?

He spun in a slow circle, his gaze coming to rest on an

opening in the hedge. Of course – the maze. He had nearly forgotten about it. Settling his hat more firmly, he entered.

Leafy green walls rose up on either side of him, too tall to peer over. Memories stirred of darting around the maze with Charlie when they were boys. He recalled that in the very center was a small pond, featuring a statue of an underdressed nymph. That had been the main attraction of the maze. Well, that, and losing Charlie's younger sister. Now she thought to turn the tables on him. He felt a smile tug at his lips.

Moving quietly, he turned – left, right, right. The same pattern again. The air was warm and heavy within the embrace of the tall hedges. A single bee buzzed lazily past his cheek.

Another minute brought him to the center. It was much as he remembered it. Just past the statue of the nymph, a bit of white cloth fluttered. Holding his breath, Edward crept forward.

"Aha!" he cried, leaping in front of the statue.

The bonnet dangled from the nymph's stone fingers, but there was no sign of Miss Price.

No sign, perhaps, but certainly a sound. He snatched the bonnet and, hands on his hips, turned toward the muffled laugh.

"You've bested me, Miss Price," he said. "But I have your bonnet. You'll have to come out to claim it."

He should have remembered she was a quick-witted girl. Several times she had neatly turned his and Charlie's tricks back on them, despite her younger age. It had been tremendously annoying at the time, but now he could appreciate her cleverness.

The hedge quivered and she emerged, pushing branches

out of her way. Edward studied her a moment. In the moonlight last night, he had not been able to see how much she had changed. She still had brown hair and eyes, her mouth a trifle too wide, her nose bearing the same, sharp slope as her brother's. Yet she looked altogether different than he remembered.

"Has staring become the fashion in London?" she asked.

Edward shook himself. "There are leaves in your hair."

"My bonnet, if you please." She held out her hand, a faint flush staining her cheeks. No doubt she was regretting the impulse that had sent her hiding in the hedge.

He handed it to her, strangely at a loss for words. From beyond the confines of the maze, he heard Charlie's voice calling his name.

Miss Price jammed the bonnet over her hair and tied the strings with quick efficiency.

"My brother's looking for you," she said. "Good afternoon, Lord Edgerton."

She turned and, without a backward glance, whisked through one of the leafy doorways and was gone.

***

Miranda pushed out of the overgrown passage on the far side of the maze, her breath still coming fast. She felt as though her heart would burst from the shame of her childish behavior. What had she been thinking, running away from Edward like that and playing foolish tricks? She had managed to – once again – humiliate herself in his eyes.

He had given her such a look and then told her she had leaves in her hair. The mortification of it scalded her cheeks.

She was not a silly young girl any more, even if he seemed to have that effect upon her. With a quick glance over her shoulder, she hastened toward the sheltering stone walls of Wyckerly. It should not be difficult to avoid him – he had been dressed for riding, his boots polished to a high sheen, his coat hugging his broad shoulders. Quite a dashing figure, just like the newspaper sketches of fashionable gentlemen taking the air in Hyde Park.

And here she was, sticky from the heat, in her third-best bonnet and drab gown. She frowned at the faded fabric. Well, it could not be helped – and it was not as though Edward's estimation of her could fall any lower. Not when she persisted in making a complete fool of herself, time and again.

From here out, she was determined to never be alone in his company. Not even for a moment.

***

Edward met up with Charlie outside the maze.

"Get lost, did you?" Charlie glanced at the hedge.

Edward cleared his throat. "Just seeing what has changed over the years."

Miranda Price had grown far beyond that simple drawing of a girl he had observed in the parlor. He had thought her plain, but the sparkle in her eyes, her wide, rosy lips, the glossy sheen of her hair – all of that combined to give a very different impression. If not of classical beauty, then of a certain prettiness, a lively spirit.

"Not much," his friend said as they strode past the flowerbeds and headed toward the stables. "And I'm glad of it. I must admit, I've missed Wyckerly. I'm a country man at heart, despite your pernicious influence."

"Wasn't it only last week that you encouraged me to stay up and watch the sunrise – with a lady on each arm?"

"Well." Charlie grinned. "I'm a quick learner. Though, as I recall, you begged off and went to bed. It was a lovely sunrise, what we could see through the smog. In my experience, country sunrises are much better, although the company is rather less sparkling."

"How long do you intend to remain at Wyckerly?" Edward asked.

"Are you offering to take me back to London once you've solved your problems here? Perhaps I want to stay longer."

Edward lengthened his stride, the gravel crunching under his boot heels. "It could be months. I spent the morning looking over the estate's books, and the figures did nothing but give me a headache."

"Did they?" Charlie gave him an astute look. "You know, my sister is quite talented in the mathematical department. She's been keeping the accounts here at Wyckerly for ages. She could assist you."

"How kind of you to offer her up like a sacrificial lamb."

Edward supposed it was a measure of his desperation that he would even consider Miss Price's assistance. But he had ever been defeated by numbers. If he had any hope of returning to London quickly and escaping his mother's matrimonial plans, he would need help sorting through the accounts.

"Miranda won't mind." Charlie waved his hand. "She's bored out of her wits – I can tell. A project like this would do her good. I'll bring her over on the morrow, after breakfast."

***

Miranda stood beside her brother on the wide front steps of Edgerton Manor. The sun lay warm on her back, and a thrush called in the woods beyond the garden, the liquid notes rising and falling.

Oh, why had she agreed to this foolish notion of Charlie's? She did not want to spend this glorious June day inside, combing ledgers for what was certainly a misplaced comma, or a random zero inserted where one ought not to be.

But Edward Havens was her brother's friend, regardless of what she thought of the man. Surely the trembling in her stomach was dislike and trepidation. She would swallow it back, help the wretched fellow, and take her leave.

Charlie blithely hammered the curved brass knocker, then gave her a bright smile. She bit her lip and listened to the echoes of the knocker fall silent.

A moment later, the butler opened the door.

"Mr. Price, Miss Price," he said, his expression impassive. "Lord Edgerton is expecting you in the study."

The butler led them down the familiar, richly paneled hallway. All too soon, they stood before the mahogany study door.

"You owe me dearly for this," she said to her brother in a low voice.

He simply grinned at her and pushed the door wide.

Inside, the earl sat behind a wide desk. His hair was disheveled, as though he had been raking his fingers through it. Account books lay open, scattered haphazardly across the desk and chairs. The cheery estate manager, Mr. Fowler, sat at a table beneath the tall windows. His eyebrows were drawn together as he perused a sheaf of papers.

"Ah," Edward said, rising when he caught sight of them. "Our mathematical genius and her entourage. Welcome. Please, make yourselves comfortable."

He heaved a stack of books off a nearby chair and offered the seat to Miranda.

"Thank you," she said.

Had he called her a genius as a compliment or a jibe? His deep blue eyes looked sincere, and a bit weary – no hint of malice sparking in their depths. Perhaps he was grateful for her assistance, after all.

"Fowler," the earl said, "ring for tea."

"Of course, my lord." The manager nodded and quietly left the room.

"Well," Charlie said, hands on his hips, "it looks like you're making rather a mess of things in here. Where shall we begin?"

The earl cocked an eyebrow. "You're planning to help, as well?"

"At least until I get bored. Then I'll switch to poetry."

Miranda muffled an unladylike snort of laughter with her gloved hand. She expected her brother wouldn't last a half hour at the figures.

But he would remain, of course. Unmarried young ladies were never left alone in the company of scandalous earls – no matter how unappealing said earls found them. She stripped off her gloves and pulled her chair closer to the desk.

"What are you working on now?" she asked.

"Last fall's rents and expenses. It's heavy going."

"Hm." She turned one of the books toward her and

studied the jotted notes and angular lines of numbers. "A good enough place to begin."

Mr. Fowler re-entered the study, followed by a maid bearing tea. Miranda poured out, and then the four of them – the earl, herself, Charlie, and the manager – settled to their task. The silence was broken only by the ruffle of pages turning, the sound of Charlie swallowing his tea.

Running one finger down the column of numbers, she could find nothing amiss. The rents seemed a bit low, but then, the old earl had likely not raised them in some time.

"Lord Edgerton," she said after some minutes, "have you earlier books, from last spring?"

Before his father had died.

The earl nodded and gestured at his estate manager. "I'm sure Mr. Fowler can find whatever you need."

The manager rose and smiled at her. "Which months would you like, Miss Price?"

"January through April, I would think."

"Here you are." He set a stack of books by her elbow. "I've gone over them twice, myself, but perhaps you'll be able to find something. Truly, I wonder if things are going astray in London, after all. I never did trust milord's solicitor."

Not knowing how to reply to that, Miranda gave him a smile and nod of thanks, then bent her head to the figures.

The sun had crawled partway across the desk when she found the first inconsistency – an oddity in the figures that had so far been quite predictable. She took a swallow of her now-cold tea and rose.

"Time for a break, I agree," Charlie said. He closed the book on his lap with a snap, and bounded up. "Any luck?"

"Possibly." Miranda turned to the earl. "Did your father

sell off any of his holdings, just before he died?"

"Not that I'm aware of." He ran one hand through his hair. "Fowler?"

The manager frowned thoughtfully. "No, my lord – not that I was aware of."

Despite his calm tone, Miranda could not help feeling that the man was lying. But what about? So far, there was no evidence of anything – except the fact that the Edgerton estate seemed to be unaccountably declining.

The numbers would show her – she had no doubt. Mathematical equations based on inaccuracy were bound for failure. Somewhere in the stacks of account books lay the answer.

The earl rose from his seat behind the desk. "Will you stay for luncheon? I've told mother you would."

"Then we can hardly decline," Charlie said. "I suppose you'll force more of this ghastly work on us this afternoon. But bribes of foodstuffs can only go so far, my friend. My sister and I are definitely returning home for supper."

A flicker of a smile crossed the earl's face. "And here I thought I'd chain you to the desk with nothing but crusts of bread to sustain you until you'd untangled my financials."

"Never," Charlie said. "It's Wordsworth for me this afternoon. I'll leave you and Miranda to your dreary numbers."

"There's a poetry in numbers, too," she said to her brother. "A pity you could never see it."

***

"Well, we survived this round," Charlie said, handing

Miranda up into the curricle for the journey home to Wyckerly. "A pity you promised to return tomorrow."

He clambered up, the vehicle dipping under his weight, and took the reins from the waiting footman. Late beams of light slanted through the trees lining the long, sweeping drive, the soil carefully kept clear of debris. The air was scented with grasses, the reminder of heat on green leaves.

Miranda threaded her gloved fingers together. "There's something odd about the accounts. In the past nine months in particular there are a large number of expenditures."

Charlie shrugged. "The storm damaged many of the tenant's cottages. A good landlord cares for such things – and Edward does, you know."

A stray sunbeam stabbed across her vision, and Miranda turned her head so that her bonnet more completely shaded her face.

"Yes, but the rents are markedly lower, too. It's as if one of the properties isn't producing anything at all." She pressed her lips together. "Something's missing."

"Then you'll find it." Charlie grinned at her. "But enough of these dry numbers. I need something to shake them out of my head. Shall we race down the lane?"

Her brother had never outgrown his love for speed. Whether it was galloping his horse or dashing a curricle along a country lane, he delighted in it.

And she must admit, she would love to feel the wind in her face, the speeding thud of the horse's hooves and the spinning curricle wheels vibrating in her chest. She had no need of clearing numbers from her thoughts, but Edward was another matter.

Perhaps it had been the dry nature of going over the

account books, but she had been unaccountably distracted by his presence. One moment she would be scanning a list of figures, the next her attention would be tangled in the strands of his hair.

It had darkened, since childhood – and she had found herself looking for the bright gold she remembered, layered among the oak and ash.

The wind whipped Miranda's bonnet ribbons, and she held to the edge of the curricle, the blurring wheel humming scant inches from her hand. Charlie's whooping laughter made her laugh in return, as the curricle hummed down the lane, faster and faster. The horse's tack clanked as Charlie flipped the reins, urging even more speed.

A sharp crack shuddered through the vehicle. Miranda cried out, the sound tearing from her throat as the seat tilted. The horse let out a high whinny and the curricle skewed sharply, one edge of the split axle stabbing into the soil.

"Miranda!" Charlie yelled.

The force of their speed flung her off the bench. There was nothing for her to grab hold of – only empty air and a confused blur of trees as she tumbled down.

She landed with a thud, then lay on the hard-packed drive, trying to catch her breath. Was she injured? She was afraid to move, to find out. But what of Charlie?

The horrible thought of him lying motionless on the dirt gave her the strength to lever herself up onto her elbows.

"Charlie?" Her voice trembled.

"Here," he said, sounding a bit breathless himself.

He had been thrown to the grassy verge, next to a spray of yellow flowers. They were incongruously bright against the dun of his coat. He slowly got to his feet and brushed off his breeches.

"Are you all right?" he asked.

"I... I think so," she said.

She sat up and made a careful inventory. All her limbs seemed to be functioning, though a deep ache pulsed in her left shoulder. When she drew in a long breath, her ribs twinged in protest.

"Can you stand?" Her brother offered his hand and gently pulled her to her feet.

She swayed, then caught her balance. Her legs felt like thin twigs beneath her skirts.

"Is Dapper unhurt?" She glanced at their horse, standing a short distance up the lane.

He was anchored by the shambles of the curricle, his chestnut head drooping. Charlie unharnessed him and led him a few paces.

"He's favoring his hind leg a bit, but I think the old fellow will be all right." He thumped the horse's muzzle, and Dapper gave him a snort.

"You're limping, too." Miranda glanced at the wreckage of their vehicle, the glossy black paint covered in dust, the broken axle giving the curricle a crazed tilt. "We must return to Edgerton Manor – Wyckerly is too far."

Her brother nodded. "Can you manage?"

She took a half-dozen careful steps. As best she could determine, she was only bruised and shaken.

"I can walk."

Gathering the horse's reins in one hand, Charlie turned back toward Edgerton Manor. "If you find you can't, we'll boost you up onto Dapper's back."

The air held the first taste of evening's chill. Miranda

glanced over her shoulder at the curricle listing in the shadows of the lane, and a shiver scraped the back of her neck. She and Charlie could have been badly injured. They were lucky to be walking away from the accident with only scrapes and bruises.

Back at the estate, Lady Edgerton greeted them with consternation. Edward dispatched servants for the doctor and to Wyckerly, and insisted that Miranda and Charlie stay the night.

"By the time Doctor Crewe arrives, it will be full dark," he said. "You'll sup with us, and the servants are preparing rooms for you. Tomorrow you may return to Wyckerly, but not before."

Charlie took it all with his usual good humor, though Miranda noticed he winced when he rose from the supper table. As for herself, she ached all over. The doctor had proclaimed nothing broken, but her ribs and shoulder throbbed terribly.

"Oh, miss." The maid shook her head as she helped Miranda out of her gown that evening. "Them bruises look right painful. I'll fetch you a compress from the kitchens, shall I?"

"That would be lovely."

Wearing a nightdress borrowed from Lady Edgerton, Miranda climbed beneath the smooth, unfamiliar sheets. She wished she were at home in her own bed, with her parents just down the hall. Instead, she must content herself with the warm, herb-scented compress wrapped about her ribs.

She woke in the night with pain radiating through her. The compress at her side was cold and damp, which would explain why she had been dreaming of a large newt curled up next to her. Miranda pushed it out of the bed, her shoulder twinging in protest at the movement.

Edgerton Manor was filled with the quiet noises of any house settling in for the night – a creak here, a squeak there – but they were not comfortable, nor familiar. Neither was the bed. She turned on her un-bruised side, then over again on to her back. She took twenty long breaths in and out, and then twenty more. No use. Sleep had fled.

At home, on the rare nights she could not sleep, she would light a candle and read by the dim light until dreaming overtook her.

Her fingertips found the candlestick in its holder beside the bed. A few coals still glowed on the hearth, shedding a faint red light against the mantel. She slipped out of bed, the carpet thick and rough beneath her bare feet, and held her candle to the coals. The banked warmth curled up against her hands as the wick flickered, then caught.

Lady Edgerton had also lent her a wrapper – blue Chinese silk, draped at the foot of the bed. Miranda put it on, drawing it carefully over her injured shoulder, then took up her candle again and surveyed the room.

There were no books. Really, it had been too much to hope for.

It was humorous, in an ironic sort of way, that once again she planned a midnight raid on the library at Edgerton Manor. At least this time she would not be sneaking through the gardens – and she would have light.

Somewhat to her disappointment, the earl did not come upon her as she browsed the shelves. At last, with a treatise on the botanical oddities of the West Indies tucked under her arm, Miranda left the library. She closed the door quietly behind her and turned to the darkened hallway.

"Miss Price." Edward's voice came out of the soft blackness.

Miranda let out a startled squeak, and the book fell to the carpet with a thud. She raised her candle, and there he was, wearing a dark dressing gown that blended with the shadows. Only his hair, his face, and his hands were visible.

"You surprised me," she said.

"My apologies. Do you intend to make a habit of skulking about my library?"

"I couldn't sleep." She bent to retrieve the book, then winced as her side and shoulder protested the movement.

In an instant, he was at her side. He scooped up the book, then gave her a concerned look. "Give me the candle – I'll escort you back to your room."

"I'm perfectly capable of carrying a candlestick, my lord."

One eyebrow rose slightly but he did not insist. He did, however keep possession of the book.

Miranda continued down the hall toward the staircase, Edward at her side. For a tall man, he was surprisingly light-footed. Of course, she should have recalled how easily he had surprised her that first time in the library.

The candle flame picked out the gilt edges of picture frames, slid over polished tabletops. She could think of nothing to say to him – and really, they did not want to be found like this, both in their nightclothes, walking the halls together. It did not look well, no matter how innocent.

"Watch the fifth tread," he said in a low voice when they reached the stairs. "It squeaks in the middle."

She nodded. How many times had he stolen out at night, that he knew the telltale noises? And what mischief could he possibly have gotten into here, in tame Dorset?

At the fifth stair, she was careful to place her feet on the outside of the step. He followed soundlessly behind her. The carpet at the top of the stairs was a different texture under her bare soles, not quite as silky as on the main floor. Three doors down she paused.

"My book, if you please."

"As long as you promise not to steal it." He glanced at the cover as he handed it over. "*Curious Flora of the West Indies.* What, no celestial geometry?"

"I ache too much to concentrate on higher mathematics." She had not meant to admit it, however.

He stepped closer to her, his fingers catching her chin. He studied her face, the barest line between his brows. Then his gaze met hers, and she was falling, falling into those deep blue pools she had sworn never to drown in.

"Miranda." Her name was a whisper on his lips.

The candle in her hand trembled, the light shivering over his gold-streaked hair. She felt suddenly caught up in the silent center of a whirlwind – furious forces on either side of her, but nothing but sweet, deep pressure within. Her breath was a faint movement of air over her lips.

Edward bent, and something tightened inside her, at her center. Her gaze dropped to his mouth as he leaned closer.

Then he shifted, his lips brushing her forehead. He stepped back, and disappointment flooded her. She had thought... she had hoped...

"Rest well," he said, his expression shuttered. "Goodnight, Miss Price."

"Wait." She held out the candlestick. "Take the candle."

"No need."

He turned and moved down the hall, a bright, silent

shadow. Four heartbeats later, he was gone.

She swallowed, her throat suddenly aching. What a fool she was.

The doorknob was cool under her hand. She twisted it, her shoulder protesting, and slipped into the room. The bed waited, patient and cold. She set the book and candle on the nightstand, all taste for reading gone.

The truth stung her tongue, like the smell of smoke from the snuffed candle. She did not hate Edward Havens – not at all. In fact, she suspected she never had, even after that dreadful day.

It took a very long time for sleep to claim her.

***

The next morning, Miranda's ribs protested as she slid out of bed, but her shoulder did not ache nearly as much. With the maid's assistance, she dressed in the blue muslin gown she had worn the day before. There was dirt ground in near the hem, more than a quick brushing-off could cure. At least it was fairly unnoticeable.

Miranda took the stairs slowly, gripping the polished banister to keep her balance. The fifth step creaked beneath her boot. It seemed she was the last to arrive in the morning room for breakfast. Edward, his mother, and Charlie were gathered about the sunny table. The silver tea service shone cheerfully, and the sideboard was filled with platters of food – kippers, toast, bacon, eggs, and fruit.

Charlie was already halfway finished with a plate of eggs. He looked in perfect health, as though curricle spills were an everyday occurrence.

"Good morning, Miranda" he said, ever chipper.

Lady Edgerton set down her cup of tea. "How are you feeling today, Miss Price? Did you sleep well?"

Miranda did not glance over at Edward. "Yes, thank you. I am much improved."

"May I fetch you a plate, Miss Price?" Edward asked. "Since your brother is too engaged with eating to offer."

"I am getting my strength back up," Charlie said. "Besides, I knew you would be gentleman enough to offer."

"I..." She lifted her shoulder, then winced at the movement. "Thank you, Lord Edgerton. Bacon, eggs, and toast if you please."

Lady Edgerton poured her a cup of tea, then handed her the delicate, rose-decorated china. Miranda stirred a lump of sugar in, the spoon clinking round the edges of the cup.

Edward set a plate before her, and she nodded her thanks. He certainly *was* acting the gentleman.

Except for his innuendos that first night he had caught her in the library, he was exceedingly well-behaved. Indeed, last night had provided ample opportunities for him to prove himself a scandalous rake – and all he had done was kiss her forehead, as though she were a child.

"Your parents will be coming to fetch you in their carriage at half eleven," Lady Edgerton said. "They wanted to rush over last night, but I directed Dr. Crewe to stop at Wyckerly and reassure them by sharing his diagnosis of you both. No need to upset the entire neighborhood."

Miranda was surprised her mother hadn't rushed over straight away. Yet... there had been that spark in her eyes when Charlie announced they would spend the day at Edgerton. Could it be that Mother harbored designs on her daughter's behalf? Toward Edward?

Ridiculous. Miranda took a swallow of tea, then chased the notion down with a bite of toast for good measure.

"We could walk home," she said, though her ribs twinged at the thought.

"Nonsense," Lady Edgerton said. "You are to rest, as Dr. Crewe instructed."

"And not in front of the account books, either," Charlie added.

Miranda shot a glance at the clock on the mantel. "But it is scarcely nine o'clock. I could easily spend an hour going over – "

"No," Edward said.

She glanced over at him, and felt a faint flush rise in her cheeks. His hair was slightly tousled, and his eyes…

Miranda pulled her attention away, and pretended to study the view outside the window. The morning light lay warm and inviting over the flowerbeds, illuminating the blue and white Canterbury bells nodding in the breeze, the pink roses sunning themselves over the arbor.

"Perhaps I will sit in the gardens, then," she said.

And if she recalled the figures from the estate books while admiring the roses, no one would be the wiser.

"Very good," Lady Edgerton said. "I will sit with you, and we can discuss the ball."

"The ball?" Miranda blinked.

"Mother." Edward crumpled up his napkin and set it on the table. "You needn't tax Miss Price with details."

"Well." His mother gave him a frosty look. "Since you won't discuss them with me…"

"That would be lovely." Miranda summoned up a smile.

"Am I to understand you are hosting a ball here?"

Lady Edgerton's blue eyes sparkled as she turned to Miranda. "A ball and a small house party, in a fortnight's time. Your family is invited, of course. Remind me to give you your official invitation before you depart this morning."

"Who else is coming?" Charlie asked, pushing his plate aside.

"From London, Lady Montfort and her daughters. And the Davenports, of course."

"Of course," Charlie echoed. He shot Edward a look, brows raised.

Miranda did not know what significance the Davenports held, but the frown on the earl's face hinted at secrets.

"The Davenports have a daughter as well?" she asked.

She was beginning to sense a pattern – one that made her oddly uncomfortable. Or perhaps that was simply her bruised ribs, aching from the strain of sitting perfectly upright.

"Yes," Lady Edgerton said with a smile. "Leticia is a lovely girl. I believe she and Edward have encountered one another about Town."

Her son shifted, his frown growing more pronounced.

"It's a veritable bouquet of young ladies," Charlie said. "Once you add Miranda in, that is."

Yes – a daisy among hothouse flowers. It was clear Lady Edgerton was hoping to find a match for Edward, a lily or an orchid to bloom companionably by his side.

"Viscount Trelling and his family will attend the events, as well," Lady Edgerton said. "So you see, we shall have quite a convivial gathering in attendance. Come, Miss Price, let us repair to the gardens. I was thinking of planning a picnic one day, and perhaps an outing to view the swans, if the weather holds. Here, take a parasol."

Lady Edgerton handed her a lace-trimmed one from the stand by the side door and, still talking, led the way out.

Miranda followed, giving up her thoughts of numbers. She did not mind passing the time with Edward's mother, and it was good to see Lady Edgerton returning to her former, sparkling self.

And truly, she understood that Edward must marry *some*one. If she had once dreamed that it might be her, well, those had been childish imaginings.

She knew better now.

***

The Havenses second-best carriage was still finer than the one Miranda's family owned. The leather seats were decently sprung – although two hours of jolting along on the country roads was enough to make anyone uncomfortable. The dark blue velvet curtains – as deep as Edward Havens's eyes – were drawn back from the now-dusty windows displaying a view of Dorset's coastline.

Indeed, the carriage was fine enough. It was the company that set Miranda's teeth on edge. Miss Trelling, who shared her bench, was a pleasant girl, but seated opposite were the Davenports. Lady Davenport seemed amiable, though she was clearly cast in the doting mama mold. Her daughter Leticia, however, was the least agreeable creature Miranda ever had the misfortune of meeting. If the ballrooms and parlors of London were full of such ladies, she was entirely happy to remain in Dorset for the rest of her life.

"I find country outings to be so quaint," Miss Davenport

said. Then her perfect blue eyes widened as she glanced across at Miranda. "Oh, do forgive me. I keep forgetting how infrequently you've been to London."

Miranda kept a smile pasted on her face, though it made her cheeks ache. "Yes, I find that the soot and din of Town doesn't agree with me. But some people are less sensitive to such things."

It had been like this for the past hour and a half – verbal slings and barbed words flying back and forth between them. Miranda felt lacerated, but she was not going to let Miss Davenport come off the winner.

"Well." Miss Davenport wrinkled her nose. "Luckily, Lord Edgerton is quite fond of London living. Once I wed the earl, we'll spend most of our time enjoying the true gentility that only is offered in Town."

Lady Davenport stirred and gave her daughter a mild glance. "Letty, do not put the cart before the horse. The earl has not yet declared his intentions toward you."

"Not yet – but I have no doubt of the outcome." Miss Davenport's smile was sparkling, but her eyes held a cold calculation.

Miranda drew her shawl more closely about her shoulders and turned her attention out the window. The green countryside appeared the same as the last time she had looked.

She would love to thwart the scheming Miss Davenport, though she had little hope of it. The young lady was beautiful, with her porcelain skin and raven-dark hair. She came of an excellent family, and seemed everything an earl would require in a wife – except for her unpleasant nature. Surely even the worst of rogues did not deserve such a wife.

Miss Trelling, a rather shy girl to begin with, had spoken

no more than two words during the entire journey, but now she gave a quiet cough.

"I believe Abbotsbury is just ahead," she said.

Although she had lived in Dorset her entire life, Miranda had never been to see the swans at Abbotsbury. A pity she had to endure the current company to do so. The carriage ride back would doubtlessly be equally unpleasant.

"Thank goodness," Miss Davenport said. "This carriage truly needs refitting. The curtains are dreadfully shabby, and leather seats have gone out of fashion."

She flicked at the seat with a gloved finger, as though the leather was old and cracked instead of supple and gleaming.

The vehicle drew to a halt, and the footman opened the doors, letting in a swath of sunshine. Miss Davenport stood immediately and stepped out, clearly accustomed to considering herself first and foremost. Both Miranda and Miss Trelling hung back, allowing Lady Davenport to step out behind her daughter.

"Have you been to Abbotsbury often?" Miranda asked.

"Yes," Miss Trelling said, dipping her bonnet so that it shaded her face. "My brother is interested in ornithology, and I accompany him to keep him out of trouble. The west dock at the lagoon is rather rickety."

Miranda nodded. Although he was a gentleman of two and twenty, Miss Trelling's older brother was not particularly suited to make his way in the world. He had always been a distant, meticulous kind of fellow. Quite the odd duck, Miranda's father called him. Considering the young man's interest in birds, the description was apt. Not that she would say as much to Miss Trelling.

They exited the carriage to find the rest of the party

gathered by the water. The Havenses other vehicle had transported Lady Edgerton, Lady Montfort, and the two Montfort daughters, Amelia and Charlotte. Edward had ridden his own horse, lucky fellow, accompanied by Charlie. The two of them were directing the footmen in unloading Lady Edgerton's picnic provisions.

From the number of baskets and parcels, it looked as if she had been planning to equip an expedition to the Continent rather than a jaunt down the coast of Dorset.

The soft June air smelled of green grass – with a pungent overtone of bird offal. Of course, the presence of hundreds of white swans bobbing on the water and clustered on the shore had an olfactory as well as visual impact. Miss Davenport sniffed and brought her kerchief to her nose.

"Heavens," she said. "How very – picturesque."

"Don't worry," Charlie said, passing by with a tablecloth bundled in his arms. "The picnic will be upwind – and you'll get used to the smell."

Miss Davenport looked faintly horrified at the thought, and Miranda could not check her smile.

"Come along," Lady Edgerton said. "We shall view the swans first."

She picked up her skirts and headed for the small dock jutting into the shallow lagoon. The birds did not seem at all vexed by having a number of people moving toward them. A few hoarse whistles disturbed the air, and one swan entered the lagoon, its neck gloriously arched, but the majority remained unperturbed.

"Look at the cygnets," Miss Trelling said. She gestured at three bits of soft gray fluff peeking from beneath their mother's wing. "Of course, you don't want to approach them.

Swans are quite defensive of their young."

Charlie and Edward joined them, having finished conveying the last of the supplies from the carriages. Further west, the footmen bustled about, preparing the picnic. Miranda wondered if there would be pickled eggs, and what the swans might think of that.

"Oh, my," Miss Davenport said, stumbling gracefully and clutching at Edward's arm. "The ground here is not terribly stable, is it?"

Clever of her, to have maneuvered close enough to catch her quarry's arm before 'losing her footing.' The girl was certainly scheming. Watching her left a sour taste in Miranda's mouth.

"Allow me to assist you," Edward said, as if it had been his intention all along.

"Miss Trelling?" Charlie appeared beside the shy young woman and, with a flourish, offered his forearm. "We wouldn't want you to turn one of those pretty ankles on this rough terrain."

"Oh…" Miss Trelling hesitantly placed her hand on Charlie's arm. "Thank you Char – er, Mr. Price."

They had known Viscount Trelling and his family for simply ages. Miranda had never quite determined if Charlie harbored a special tenderness for Henrietta Trelling, or if he was simply being kind.

Without an escort of her own, Miranda folded her arms and marched ahead to the ruffled water. The grass under her feet was lumpy and tussocked, but certainly not hazardous enough to warrant grabbing helplessly on to a gentleman's arm.

The blue sky was echoed in the lagoon, and the hills rose

along the side like a rucked-up green-and-brown blanket. Off the end of the dock a swan spread its wings and, with a great beating and splashing, began to ascend. Its feet trod the water and then the huge white wings lifted it into the sky, the air whistling rhythmically through its feathers.

Miranda stepped onto the weathered boards. Partway down, a loose plank see-sawed under her foot, and she quickly moved away from the edge – the rickety dock Miss Trelling had mentioned.

"How very rustic!" Miss Davenport said as she and Edward approached. She still clung like a limpet to his arm. "Why, you look perfectly at home here, Miss Price. How pleasant this must be for you."

Edward frowned down at Miss Davenport's ornately decorated bonnet, but said nothing.

"Indeed," Miranda said. "I've always thought fresh air and sunshine helped combat the sickly look I've observed so often in Londoners. After some time, it will work its wonders on you as well, Miss Davenport."

The young lady sniffed, then turned pointedly away. Charlie and Miss Trelling joined Miranda on the dock, and her brother shook his head.

"You're a rascal," he said to her in an undertone.

"I can't help it."

"Well, try. She's a guest, after all."

Miranda refrained from pointing out that the Davenports were not *her* guests. It was simply impossible to bear Miss Davenport in silence – although Miss Trelling seemed to manage well enough. Indeed, Miss Davenport had turned her attention to the other young lady.

"What an interesting color your gown is," Miss

Davenport said. "Is mud-brown the fashion in the country? I had no idea."

A flush bloomed on Miss Trelling's cheeks, but she said nothing, only stared down at the weathered boards beneath their feet.

Charlie cleared his throat, and Miranda raised her brows at him. Was her brother going to say something after just scolding her for doing the same?

"Things are different in London," he managed.

Disappointment folded around Miranda. Was no one going to stand up to the horrible Miss Davenport?

"Oh my, yes." Miss Davenport laughed – a sound that rang artificially over the water. "A change is so refreshing. For a short period of time, that is. One wouldn't want to become accustomed to the country. As soon as the ball is over, Mother and I will be returning to Town. With a happy announcement, I hope."

She squeezed Edward's arm, her eyes bright with greedy expectation.

Miranda's gaze slipped to Edward. How could he possibly be contemplating marrying this girl? She was everything dreadful.

He stared across the water, his expression distant.

"Well, Miss Davenport, while you are here, I encourage you to immerse yourself in the experience," Miranda said. "After all, many peers enjoy repairing to their country estates for part of the year. Oh, look!" She stepped closer to the edge of the dock and made a show of glancing at the empty water. "The most lovely little sight – a cygnet perched just behind its mother's neck. Do come see, Miss Davenport."

With a toss of her head, Miss Davenport let go of

Edward's arm and came to stand beside Miranda.

"Where? I don't see anything."

"They went around the corner. Perhaps if you lean forward a bit..."

Miranda lifted her right foot, where she had been pinning down the loose board Miss Davenport stood on. The wood tilted, and Miss Davenport let out a shriek.

"Help!" she cried, teetering on the edge.

She flailed, grabbing hold of Miranda's arm. Edward lunged to catch them, but it was too late – Miss Davenport tumbled off the dock, taking Miranda with her.

They hit with a splash. The water was cool, and muddy this close to the shore, with a few bits of white down curling on the surface. Miranda landed on her side, her hand touching the smooth slime at the bottom before she righted herself.

"Help! Help!" Miss Davenport cried.

Another splash signaled Edward's entry into the lagoon. He caught Miranda's elbow, and with his steady support, she got her feet under her and stood. The water came to just above her knees, and her gown clung wetly to her. A rivulet ran down her cheek. She wiped at it with her soggy glove, which did not improve matters.

"Are you all right?" he asked. "Your shoulder?"

She lifted her shoulders in a quick, exploratory shrug. "Well enough."

"That was a foolish thing to do." He let go of her arm. "Stay calm, Miss Davenport," he called, making his way to where the young lady persisted in flailing about.

He managed to pull her to her feet, only to have her shriek again and throw herself at him. The two of them tumbled back into the water, and Miranda began to laugh.

What a comedy of errors. She supposed everyone in the lagoon deserved what they had gotten.

From the dock, Charlie grinned at her. Miss Trelling's lips twitched, then opened out into a wide, genuine smile.

"I hope the leeches haven't grown too large yet," Charlie called down.

"Leeches?" Miss Davenport screeched.

She seemed to be trying to climb up Edward, who gallantly stood his ground. The continual racket of Miss Davenport was upsetting the swans. A dozen of them took to the air, adding to the din with their splashing take-offs and thrum of vibrating wings.

Miranda waded to shore, her boots squelching uncomfortably with each step. Edward followed, bearing Miss Davenport in his arms.

Lady Edgerton hurried up, with Lady Davenport right behind.

"Edward," his mother said, "is everyone well?"

"Get them off!" cried Miss Davenport, waving her legs wildly beneath her sodden skirts. "The horrid things, remove them at once!"

Edward stumbled the last few feet and dumped her onto solid ground.

"There are no leeches," he said. "Compose yourself, Miss Davenport. We are unharmed, Mother – if a bit damp. I believe Miss Davenport would like to return to the carriage."

"My poor girl." Lady Davenport went and laid her arm around her daughter's shoulders. "What a dreadful accident. How did it happen?"

"Miss Davenport was immersing herself in the country experience," Miss Trelling said. There was a definite spark of humor in her eyes. "They were admiring the color of my gown, and thought to apply it to their own. The bottom of the lagoon seemed a suitable choice."

Charlie laughed outright at that, and even Edward looked about to smile.

"I don't find it amusing in the least," Lady Davenport said. "Come along, darling."

Miss Davenport stopped her sniffling long enough to shoot Miranda a dagger-edged glare. Their acquaintance had just been elevated to a new level of enmity.

***

Three days later, Lady Edgerton hosted a dinner party. The long table was decked with snowy linens and gold-edged plates. Candelabra set at close intervals added a warm glow, though pale evening light still seeped in through the Palladian windows lining the side of the dining room.

Miranda was relieved to be seated far down the table from Miss Davenport – even though it placed the young lady next to Edward. Still, it was none of her concern whom he chose to court. She took a sip of champagne, the bubbles tickling her nose, and watched Charlie, who was seated beside her, flirt with Miss Trelling on his other side.

Was he in earnest, or simply entertaining himself by making Miss Trelling blush and laugh? She'd hate to think her brother had become a rake – though if he had, it was likely Edward Havens's fault.

Miranda looked to the head of the table, surprised to find the earl watching her. Their eyes met, held, and a curious, breathless sensation shivered over her. Then Miss Davenport patted his shoulder, and he turned to her in reply.

For the next five minutes Miranda shot covert glances at him, between bites of the poached fish on her plate. He did not look her way again.

After the servants had removed the last course with a quiet clinking of plates and cutlery, Lady Edgerton stood and clapped her hands twice.

"Attention, dear guests," she said. "We will be observing the more informal country tradition of repairing to the drawing room – ladies and gentlemen together – for some entertainment."

"No sitting about swilling port," Miranda said to Charlie.

"A pity. I was hoping to discuss the gruesome details of pheasant hunting with the other gentlemen." Her brother gave her a cheerful smile. "At least I have pleasant company."

He did not mean herself, of course. Instead, he held his arm out to Miss Trelling. And then the scoundrel offered his other arm to the older Montfort daughter, Amelia, on the way out of the dining room. Miss Davenport was, as usual, clamped onto Edward's side.

Being one of a half-dozen young ladies with only two gentlemen in attendance was becoming rather tiresome. Miranda hesitated at the dining room threshold. If she snuck off to look at account books in the study, would anyone notice? Behind her, the servants blew out the candles, gray tendrils of smoke scrolling into the air.

"Miranda!" Her mother paced back down the hallway from the direction of the drawing room, a determined look in her eyes. "There you are."

No escape now. Miranda let out an invisible sigh.

"Yes. Here I am."

In West Dorset. Forever.

Which, if she could spend all her time at Wyckerly studying mathematics, would not be such a bad thing. It was only the intrusion of rakish earls and scheming misses that made her want to run away.

The drawing room at Edgerton Manor was decorated in warm red and ivory. Velvet-upholstered chairs and divans were arranged into comfortable groupings. Charlie was ensconced between Amelia Montfort and Miss Trelling on a low sofa. The older ladies, along with Miranda's father, sat in a cluster of chairs near the corner. Edward had taken an armchair, and Miss Davenport occupied the chair next to it. The nearby divan stood empty, and Miss Davenport's face held a hint of disgruntlement, as though she had expected to settle cozily beside Edward there, and he had thwarted her plans. The back half of the room was dedicated to musical instruments: a pianoforte, a harp, and an assortment of flutes – some of which looked completely unplayable.

Miranda took a seat on the divan near Edward. Miss Davenport shot her a narrow-eyed glance, and then pointedly pulled her chair an inch closer to Edward's.

"Now that we are all assembled," Lady Edgerton said with a nod at Miranda, "it is time for the entertainments to begin. I know this group holds many and diverse talents, and one could not find a more agreeable audience to perform in front of. Who would like to go first?"

There was an uncomfortable silence, and then Charlie jumped to his feet.

"I shall recite some poetry," he said. "Lord Byron should do nicely."

The Montfort girls let out identical sighs – clearly the

poet was high in their romantic estimation.

Charlie strode to the center of the red-and-white patterned carpet and struck a pose – one arm cocked before him, his chin jutting up in what was likely meant to be a heroic fashion. He cleared his throat and began.

> *"She walks in beauty, like the night*
> *Of cloudless climes and starry skies;*
> *And all that's best of dark and bright*
> *Meet in her aspect and her eyes:*
> *Thus mellow'd to that tender light*
> *Which heaven to gaudy day denies."*

From the corner of her eye, Miranda saw Miss Davenport smooth back her raven-dark hair with one hand and send Edward a wide-eyed glance – no doubt implying she was also the "best of dark and bright" referenced in the poem. He gave no sign that he noticed her preening, and a small, unworthy gladness kindled in Miranda's chest.

Miss Trelling, she observed, was blushing prettily, her gaze fastened on Charlie, her eyes shining.

> *"And on that cheek, and o'er that brow,*
> *So soft, so calm, yet eloquent,*
> *The smiles that win, the tints that glow,*
> *But tell of days in goodness spent,*
> *A mind at peace with all below,*
> *A heart whose love is innocent!"*

Miranda suspected Miss Davenport's heart was far from innocent, and her days were certainly not spent in goodness.

As for a mind at peace? She herself was decidedly not possessed of one.

Charlie finished with a flourishing bow, and the younger ladies applauded with great vigor.

"Thank you, sir," Lady Edgerton said. "That was a most agreeable diversion. Since you were the first to grace us with your talent, you may select the next performer."

"Hm." Charlie folded his arms and made a show of looking the guests over.

His gaze landed on Miss Trelling, who blushed even more deeply and gave her head the slightest of shakes. Either the young lady was too painfully shy, or she had no party piece to perform in company. In a rather gentlemanly move, Charlie let her go. He continued to circle the room.

"I choose... Miss Davenport," he said.

"Oh my." She gave an artificial-sounding giggle and rose from her chair. "I believe I shall play upon the harp this evening. Lord Edgerton has remarked that my rendition of 'The Minstrel Boy' is particularly memorable."

She bestowed a simpering smile on Edward.

"Indeed," he said. "I still recall your performance at the Forsythe's musicale some months ago."

Miranda's brows rose. Was Miss Davenport truly such an accomplished musician? She shot a look at her brother, whose mouth had the tucked-in expression that meant he was smothering his laughter. Interesting.

Miss Davenport seated herself at the harp and played a glissando. The notes rang true and clear through the room, a waterfall of sound. She plucked out a simple introduction, then opened her mouth and began to sing.

It was immediately apparent that Miss Leticia Davenport

had no notion of proper pitch. Her voice warbled and wavered, sometimes alighting upon the melody, most often straying from it. The Montfort girls watched her, their eyes wide. Charlie was biting his lip, and Edward looked particularly stoic.

Even Miranda's father winced when Miss Davenport attempted the high notes, and he was notoriously immune to such things. Lady Edgerton had a strained smile pasted upon her face, but Lady Davenport smiled and nodded in time, seeming blissfully unaware of her daughter's lack of musicality. Either she shared the same affliction, or her daughter could do no wrong in her eyes. Or both.

When at last the ballad was ended, the listeners clapped loudly – mostly from relief that the song was over.

"Oh, thank you," Miss Davenport dipped into a polished curtsy. "Shall I play another?"

"No, no," their hostess said. "Perhaps later. We must give everyone a turn."

"Very well." Miss Davenport walked over to Edward's chair and placed a hand on his shoulder. "I choose you, Lord Edgerton."

Heavens, she was obvious.

"I have no talent to share," he said.

"Nonsense." Charlie, a mischievous light in his eyes, snagged three polished red apples from a bowl of fruit on the nearby end table. "Stand up, Edward."

Edward rose, possibly more to avoid Miss Davenport's touch than to comply with Charlie's demand.

"Everyone is advised to duck when needed," Edward said, his tone dry.

Gathering up her skirts, Miss Davenport hastily took her

seat.

"Nonsense," Charlie said. "I haven't lost my skill at it."

The two men met face-to-face in the center of the carpet. Charlie handed Edward one of the apples, and they pivoted to stand with their backs to one another.

"One. Two, three," Charlie said, measuring each number with a step.

At the number five, they halted, turned, and Charlie flung his apples at Edward. Miss Davenport gasped, and Miranda smiled. She scooted down the divan, so that the fruit bowl was closer to hand.

Edward fired his own apple into the air, deftly caught Charlie's, then spun them back around. A brief, sunny memory flashed through Miranda of sitting on the lawn at Wyckerly and laughing as they dropped and fumbled potatoes in their quest to perfect their juggling. It had been Charlie's idea, of course. There had been jugglers at the local fair that summer, and he was determined to master the art – and drag everyone around him into it as well.

"Four!" Charlie called.

Miranda chose an apple and watched carefully. As soon as Charlie's hands were empty, she tossed it to him. It had been her role that entire month to throw potatoes into the fray, and she'd been eager to fulfill it since it put her in company with Edward.

Red blurred back and forth, both men sure and confident in their throws and catches.

"Five," Charlie said, sounding a touch breathless.

There were no more apples in the bowl, but a nice round quince would do. Miranda flung it into the mix, and the Montfort girls oohed appreciatively as Charlie caught it. The air was filled with flying fruit.

"I beg you not to make applesauce in my drawing room," Lady Edgerton said.

"Right," Edward said. "Three. Two. One."

He and Charlie halted in unison, an apple in each hand. The quince thudded to the floor, and Edward's mother let out a sigh of relief.

"Bravo," Miranda said, applauding wildly.

Charlie grinned, and Edward looked a bit happier about the eyes. Or perhaps it was his hair, tousled from exertion, that made him seem more carefree.

"What an unusual exhibition," Miss Davenport said. "I had no notion."

"Lord Edgerton is a man of hidden talents," Charlie said. "You ought to see him tame snakes and teach them to dance. Quite the dab hand."

Miss Davenport blinked, and Miranda laughed outright. "Forgive my brother," she said. "He fancies himself a wit."

"And do you have any unusual talents, Miss Price?" Miss Davenport asked, sounding as if she expected Miranda to unveil something more suited to the circus than the drawing room.

"I play the pianoforte," Miranda said.

Edward deposited the fruit back into the bowl on the table next to her, and gave her the briefest flash of a smile.

"Then I choose you to be the next performer," he said, holding out his hand.

She took it and stood, conscious of the warmth of his touch – and the narrow-eyed look Miss Davenport sent her. Quickly, she made her way to the pianoforte and settled at the bench.

"What will you play?" Lady Edgerton asked.

"Bach – the Invention number Eight." She loved the measured, mathematical paces of his compositions, the way the melodies turned and mirrored one another, like perfect sums in balance.

Miranda set her hands on the keyboard and began to play. Everything else fell away – sun-dappled memories and the bittersweet ache in her heart for what might have been, the iciness in Miss Davenport's blue eyes, the prospect of unchanging years spread before her.

There were only the notes, each one falling precisely as it should, as satisfying as an equation, as perfect as the movements of the planets scribed across the sky.

***

Miranda rubbed at her nose, and turned the page of the ledger book. She had coaxed Charlie to spend the afternoon with her in Edward's study. They both knew this was her last chance at finding the answers to the problem of the Edgerton estate's books. Tonight was the grand ball.

Tonight, everything would change.

And so she had stared for hours at the accounts, until her eyes were numb. The paper beside her was full of worked and scribbled-out sums, and still she was no closer to finding any solutions. Frustrated, she wound a stray strand of hair about her fingers and yanked on it.

Her brother dozed, oblivious, in the plush armchair nearby, a book of poetry open on his lap. He was without a doubt the laziest poet she had ever seen. In fact, he had yet to compose a bit of verse, though he laid claim to the title.

With a deep breath, Miranda pushed back the chair and stood. Her footsteps muffled by the thick green-and-gold Aubusson carpet, she went to the bookshelves. Rows of neatly-bound ledger books lined the shelves, arranged by year. The Earls of Edgerton had been a meticulous bunch. She skimmed her fingertips along the spines, feeling the bumping, orderly pattern of life inscribed within each volume.

The pattern changed, as her fingers fell into a dip. One of the books was pushed further back than its neighbors. Miranda took hold of the top and slid it out.

"Miss Price." The voice was loud and cheery.

She whirled, the ledger still in her hand, to see the estate manager, Mr. Fowler, at the doorway.

In his chair, Charlie gave a snort, and woke.

"What time is it?" he asked, his voice blurry with sleep.

"Half three," Mr. Fowler said. He was still watching Miranda.

Charlie closed the book on his lap with a snap, and jumped to his feet. "Half three? The ball begins at seven. Miranda, we must go immediately."

"Yes, you must." Mr. Fowler opened the door wide.

"I have plenty of time to dress," she said. The ledger in her hand called to her.

The estate manager went over to Miranda, looking like a rotund crow in his plain black suit. Without asking, he lifted the book from her grasp and stuck it back on the shelf.

"Wait," she said.

"Now miss, we wouldn't want you to be late for the ball. You've done so much here already – but you young folk need time to enjoy yourselves. No need to keep fretting about the earl's estate."

"But this is the last – "

"Come, Miranda," Charlie said. "You know Mother will be fretting. Even if you think you'll be ready for the ball, she'll need your assistance."

Miranda folded her arms. She did not want to dress for the grand ball, where Leticia Davenport would no doubt prod Edward to declare his intentions, and then spend the evening gloating and preening. No – Miranda wanted to stay here in the study and solve the mystery of the estate's finances. Especially as she would not be welcome at Edgerton Manor once Leticia was established as Edward's betrothed. Her final chance to help Edward was slipping through her fingers.

"Best be off with you," Mr. Fowler said, his eyes bright.

"We're going," Charlie said, taking Miranda by the elbow and guiding her to the door.

She glanced back at the shelves, marking the placement of the ledger she wanted to examine. During the ball, she would slip away and return to the study. Surely after the grand announcement, her presence would not be missed.

***

"You look splendid, darling," Lady Edgerton said as Edward entered the sitting room.

She rose in a rustle of blue taffeta skirts and lily-scented perfume to bestow a kiss on his cheek. The evening sun slanted through the tall windows, illuminating the strands of silver in her fair hair. Still, she was looking improved. Her smiles came more easily, and some of the shadows had lifted from her eyes. The house party had been successful in that, if nothing else.

He, on the other hand, did not feel splendid – not in the least – but he summoned a smile for his mother. His cravat was tied too tightly, his coat squeezed his shoulders as if it were a size too small, and his boots pinched his toes.

This evening he would fully step into the role of earl, as he ought.

He'd had no success untangling the estate's finances, but at least he could secure a bride. The month would not be an utter failure, no matter the weight that lodged in his chest at the thought of shouldering his next, inevitable duty.

He would propose to Leticia Davenport, ensuring that the long line of Dorset Edgertons remained unbroken.

"How I have longed for this day," his mother said, taking his hand and drawing him to sit beside her on the gold-upholstered divan. "Ever since Lady Davenport was delivered of a daughter when you were six years of age, we had hoped… well, our two families have always been close, as you know."

"Yes." The word stuck in his throat. He shifted, trying to keep the late sun from stabbing unpleasantly into his eyes. "I am pleased to make you happy, Mother."

He was able to do this – to help her long-imagined dreams come true. And though there were other prospects back in London, Miss Davenport was the most obvious choice for his bride.

Lady Edgerton tilted her head, a curious expression crossing her features. "But are you not making yourself happy, as well?"

"Happy enough."

Although his parents had been deeply in love, he had seen any number of marriages where the husband and wife simply tolerated one another. As long as there was a modicum of courtesy, he and Leticia Davenport could manage. Indeed, if his mother had not loved his father so dearly, his death would not have taken such a toll on her. There were reasons not to love one's spouse too much.

"Hey-o!" a voice called from the hallway.

Never one to stand on ceremony or wait for such things as the butler to announce him, Charlie Price strode into the room.

"Mr. Price – welcome," Lady Edgerton said. "You have arrived early. Is the rest of your family with you?"

Charlie bowed over her hand. "You are a vision of loveliness this evening, Lady Edgerton. As for my mother and sister, they'll be along later in the carriage. Father is pleading his gout, as usual, and staying home. At any rate, I wanted a quick word with Edward before the festivities began."

"Of course." Lady Edgerton rose. "I'll go attend to the last-minute details while you two have your chat."

She bustled out of the sitting room, and Edward raised a brow at his friend.

"Well?" he said.

Charlie folded his arms. "Are you actually going to go through with this?"

"With what, hosting a ball?"

"With asking Leticia Davenport to be your bride. Really, Ed, we've both done foolish enough things, but this..." Charlie shook his head.

Doubt made Edward's words more forceful than he wanted. "I have responsibilities now – serious ones. You may continue on your wastrel ways, Charlie, but that path is no longer for me."

Damn, he sounded like some old prune in the House of Lords, not the carefree rogue he had imagined himself to be for years to come. Before his father died.

"I understand that," Charlie said. "But can you truly imagine leg-shackling yourself to that harpy for your entire life? You'll be miserable."

Edward turned and began to pace, hands gripped behind his back. Darkness gathered in the corners of the room as the sun descended. From somewhere deeper in the house, he heard the shriek of a violin tuning up.

"She's the best choice I have." His voice was tight.

"Come now. What about Miss Aubrey?"

"Too young."

"Miss Smythe?"

"Too ordinary, and her mother is a gorgon."

"Miss – "

"See here." Edward rounded on his friend. "None of them are here, none of them are a match guaranteed to make my mother happy, and none of them would be any better, or any worse, than marrying Miss Davenport."

"I'm sure she'd be gratified to hear that." Charlie shook his head. "Isn't there anyone else?"

For a moment, Miranda's mischievous brown eyes and over-wide mouth flashed through Edward's mind. But that was a ridiculous notion. Not only was she Charlie's younger sister, she had made it clear she held him in the utmost contempt.

At least Miss Davenport professed to admire him. Whether she liked him or his title more, it was difficult to tell, but in either case she would do well enough.

"No one," Edward said.

A shadow crossed Charlie's face, quickly gone.

"Well then," he said, in a semblance of his usual cheerful voice. "Good luck and all that. I suppose I'll see you about London."

"Certainly."

And although Miss Davenport did not seem particularly fond of the Price family, Charlie was his oldest friend. He would not cut the man because of the whims of his soon-to-be betrothed.

***

Miranda stood at the edge of the ballroom, pretending to admire the decorations. Blue oriental vases overflowing with pale roses were arranged along the walls, and the candles set in the high chandeliers shone a warm golden light over the dancing couples, the crystal facets glimmering in the last of the twilight. On the dais at the far end of the dance floor, the orchestra Lady Edgerton had hired provided tuneful music for the score of dancers stepping the pattern of the quadrille.

Despite herself, Miranda watched Edward dancing with Leticia Davenport. The light glinted off the gold streaks in his hair, and he moved purposefully yet gracefully through the paces of the dance, cutting a striking figure in his dark blue coat and polished boots.

Miss Davenport clung to his arm whenever the quadrille required them to touch. Her cheeks were flushed, and her lavender silk gown rather low cut for the country – but perhaps baring that much bosom was fashionable in Town.

It was hot and noisy, the sound of conversation and laughter sawing against Miranda's nerves. She folded one arm tightly across her ribs, her breath pricking her lungs as if the air was filled with tiny pins.

Edward had not yet made any announcement – but she could not bear to remain another moment in the ballroom. Charlie could tell her later all about the joyous betrothal.

Miranda whirled and pushed through the door leading into the hallway. It was blessedly cool and quiet, old portraits gazing stolidly down at her as she sped along the dark-paneled hall toward the study. There was solace in numbers – there always had been. And perhaps she would at last find an answer, though she had no notion why an old ledger would contain any solutions.

Taking a taper from the hall, she pushed open the study door. The wavering candlelight fell across the wide, now-familiar desk. There was a candle holder there, and she quickly deposited her light before hot wax dripped onto her hand.

She moved to the shelves and studied the row of books. Had it been that one, or the one next to it? Unsure, she pulled out three and laid them on the desk.

The first one, dated *1782*, held no secrets. After ten minutes, Miranda laid it aside. The second, from the previous year, was more of the same – rows of figures in a precise hand, paired with descriptions of crops and rents, repairs and improvements.

Sighing, she closed the ledger and rubbed her forehead. There was nothing to be gained here. She ought to return to the ballroom, smile when she heard the news of the betrothal, and leave Edward Havens to sort out his own finances. It was none of her concern.

The candle flame flickered as a shadow paused in the doorway. Miranda rose to her feet, her pulse pounding high in her throat.

"Who's there?" she asked, her voice ending in a squeak.

"It's me," Edward said, stepping into the room. "But what are you doing here? Why aren't you at the ball?"

"I..." She gestured to the ledger books on the desk.

He shook his head, then held out his hand. "Though I know you prefer numbers to dancing, I insist you return. Come, Miranda."

"I really don't – "

"Don't dance? I promise I won't bite."

He paced over to her, stopping too close for comfort. She smelled the faint spice of him, felt the warmth of his body where it nearly brushed hers. Slowly, he brought his hand up and drew one finger down her cheek.

Sparks trailed from that touch, and she had to close her eyes.

"What are you doing?" she asked, from the safety of that darkness.

"Kissing you."

She caught her breath, trying not to tremble. She ought to stop him. She ought to open her eyes and slip out from between him and the desk. Yet somehow she could not.

"Edward – "

"Shh."

He set his finger over her lips, then stroked it back and forth, making her shiver. His touch dropped to her chin and he tilted her face up. His breath feathered against her mouth, and then his lips were there, warm and firm over hers. Heat flashed over her as his tongue tipped out to trace the seam of her lips.

She swayed, suddenly dizzy with yearning, and he pulled

her against him. One arm slid around her back, holding her. Her hands moved up to his broad shoulders and she clung to that solidity while everything spun about her.

He gently coaxed her mouth open, his tongue swirling in as though he were tasting the sweetest honey. A moan escaped her, and he held her even more tightly in response. Sensations rampaged through her, coiling sweet and hot at her center.

She loved Edward Havens. She always had. While he…

Miranda could barely force herself to bring her hands between them, to push him away. But she must.

"Stop," she gasped, pulling her lips from his. "Edward, please."

He lifted his head, and his arm loosened, although he still held her.

"How could you?" she asked, bitterness uncurling like a weed in her heart.

He smiled, slow and lazy. "You're quite kissable."

"I don't mean that! How could you kiss me *now*, on the very eve of your betrothal to another? You truly are an appalling rake."

She ought to slap him, but she could not manage the anger for it – not with the aftermath of his kiss still trembling her senses.

"I…" Something flashed in his eyes, shame or regret. He released her and stepped stiffly away. "You're correct. My apologies. The fact that I find you attractive is no excuse."

Now the first coals of anger began to heat. "Attractive? Don't feel the need to lie. If you are regretting the idea of asking for Miss Davenport's hand, pray do not use me as the instrument of that regret. I know exactly what you think of me."

His expression shuttered. "And what is that?"

She knotted her hands in the folds of her skirt as the memory of that dreadful afternoon five years ago seared her thoughts.

"Certainly you remember," she said.

She would never forget. She had been coming down to the parlor at Wyckerly, eagerly anticipating another outing with her brother and his friend, their neighbor Edward Havens. Edward, whose fair hair and deep blue eyes made her giddy, whose smiles and clever words she savored in memory, over and over.

"So," she had heard Charlie say, "What do you think of my sister?"

Heart pounding, she had paused outside the door, breathless to hear how her hero would reply. Did he, *could* he, hold her in some esteem? The moment had stretched as she hovered, waiting. She still recalled it with perfect clarity – the dust motes hanging in the air, the smell of lilacs and lemon polish, the uncomfortably tight fit of her boots.

Then Edward had spoken, and all her delight had come crashing down.

She stared at him now, his face half-shadowed in the flickering candle light.

"Let me refresh your memory," she said. "You said I was *regrettably bookish and plain, with very little to recommend me apart from an annoying tendency to interfere where not wanted.*"

The words were burned into her soul. With those few sentences, her girlish yearnings had been shattered, twisted into a sour reflection of her own shortcomings.

His eyes widened. "That was years ago. You've changed."

"Not significantly." She swallowed back bitter tears. "Now, if you will excuse me, I shall leave your study, and you, in peace."

She brushed past him, trying not to show how her hands shook. He did not try to stop her, did not catch her arm or call her back as she fled.

Returning to the ballroom was out of the question. No, she needed air, and quiet, and time to purge her memory of that terrible, wonderful kiss.

Edward had not meant anything by it – she understood that, deep inside. Yet part of her still wanted to believe he had kissed her because she was *herself*, Miranda Price, bookish and plain and interfering as she might be.

Not simply because she was anyone but Miss Davenport.

Vision blurred by unshed tears, she hurried along the hall and pushed open the side door leading into the garden. The night breeze cooled her flushed cheeks, and the dimness enfolded her. Only a last bit of twilight hung silver in the western sky. From the forest beyond, a bird called once, twice, then fell silent. The flowers were all closed, except for the roses. Miranda crossed her arms and tried to take a deep breath. It took three tries before she could inhale past the tightness in her chest.

She would stay out here, in the dusk garden, until she had composed herself. Then she would find Charlie and tell him she felt unwell and was leaving. Yes – that was the best course. She could not remain here, could not watch as Leticia Davenport paraded her conquest about the ballroom.

Especially not with the memory of Edward's kiss still tingling her lips. Much as she tried, she knew it was a kiss she would never forget.

***

Edward's head buzzed, and he ran one hand through his hair, tugging at the roots. What the devil had possessed him to kiss Miranda?

Had his time in London truly changed him into the jaded rake she believed him to be?

No. He'd taken leave of his senses tonight, but it was not from depravity. And, despite her accusations, he did not want to rush out and kiss any woman who presented herself. Only Miranda Price – who took everything he thought he knew and turned it on its head.

He dimly recalled the conversation with Charlie she'd described. He had been teasing, when he'd said such things of Miranda – though there had been a kernel of truth to his words. Still, it had not been kind. Casting his mind back, he remembered that Charlie had punched him in the shoulder and called him an idiot. Edward had apologized, and thought no more of it. That Miranda had been eavesdropping never occurred to him.

He tugged at his hair again. What had his careless, harmful words been?

That she was bookish – true enough. It was a mild insult. However, since encountering any number of empty-headed misses in London, he'd learned to value a woman with some learning and intelligence. And hadn't Miranda done her best to try and sort out whatever was wrong with the estate's finances? She certainly had a better sense for figures than he did.

He had called her plain – which had also seemed true.

She was a country miss, nothing like the fashionably desirable ladies in Town. Yet he'd grown strangely fond of her wide, rosy mouth, the light in her brown eyes, the particular arrangement of features that made her uniquely Miss Miranda Price.

So, not plain – any more than a refreshing glass of water was plain compared to an overly-sweet cup of punch. He knew now which was the more quenching.

And the tendency to tag along where not wanted? That was the province of younger sisters – and the one thing that had undeniably changed in Miss Miranda Price. In fact, he suspected it had on that very day five years ago, as a result of her overhearing his cruelly casual words.

She had changed, in part – but the truth was he had changed more.

"There you are, my lord!" a voice exclaimed from the doorway. "I was wondering where you'd hidden yourself."

Edward glanced up, to see Leticia Davenport standing at the threshold. She held a small lamp which cast odd shadows on her features and made her pale gown appear ghostly.

"Miss Davenport – my apologies for worrying you. Let me escort you back to the ballroom." He offered his arm.

He would deposit Leticia back in company, then go find Miranda. He owed her an apology, long overdue.

Miss Davenport ignored his arm and pushed past him into the study, setting her lamp on the desk next to Miranda's candle.

"Edward, you know I would come to find you. Though you might have chosen a more obvious spot. I've been looking for ages."

What if she'd seen him kissing Miranda? He half-wished

she had. What a difference a few moments could make in a man's life.

A cold knowledge settled in his stomach. Leticia was here for one thing – to secure his proposal of marriage. He even had the ring in his pocket, a diamond-and-pearl engagement ring that had belonged to his grandmother. Earlier that afternoon, his mother had presented it to him with a happy light in her eyes. What could he do except take the damned thing?

He slipped his hand into his coat to make sure the ring was still there. It lay cool and smooth under his fingers, but he could not bring himself to draw it out.

Leticia set her hands to her hips and gave him a petulant look. "Well? I'm waiting. We both know what's to happen now."

"Miss Davenport…" The words dried in his throat.

All he could think of were Miranda's lips, warm and pliant beneath his. Her quick, dry wit and the glossy sheen of her brown hair. The way she had hidden from him in the maze – the bright flashes of mischief she could never quite conceal. Good Lord, she had even pushed Leticia Davenport into the lagoon at Abbotsbury, and then laughed at herself when she'd fallen in as well.

Leticia scowled – a look that pulled her mouth into a thin, unbecoming line. "Really, Edward, must I do everything? Ahem. It would give me great pleasure if you would do me the honor of – "

"Wait."

Leticia Davenport was showing her true colors, now that she believed she had the bird in her hand. What a fool he'd been, trying to ignore the truth of her nature. He could not share his life with this woman.

"Wait?" she said. "I have been doing nothing but wait for the last three months! If you do not speak the words *now*, then I will be forced to ensure we are discovered in a compromising position."

"You have already tried that, as I recall."

He ought to have heeded his instincts and stayed far away from Leticia Davenport. If only his mother was not so fond of the prospect of them being wed.

It was a near thing, but he had finally come to his senses. He could not live for his mother's happiness. Only his own.

There was a wild look about Leticia's eyes now. "I shall scream."

He took a step toward her, ready to clap his hand across her mouth if necessary. No doubt she would bite.

The air was split by a woman's cry for help. Edward stared at Leticia, but she looked equally astonished. The scream had not come from her – but it had come from close by. And he recognized that voice.

Miranda!

***

In the quiet peace of the garden, Miranda's thoughts slowly found some calm. She was not losing Edward – she had never had him in the first place. Life would continue exactly the same, except that she would no longer pore over the gossip rags for mention of the Earl of Edgerton. And if her pillow was wet with tears every night, well, they would dry by morning and none the wiser.

With a final, deep breath, she squared her shoulders and

prepared to re-enter the mansion.

"Here now, miss," a cheery voice said from out of the night. "Fancy meeting you in the garden. Alone."

"Mr. Fowler?" She stepped back toward the manor as a round, dark figure emerged from the shadows.

"You oughtn't be taxing your pretty little head any further with the estate's business. It's not for a woman to do."

"I assure you, I have no further interest in the Edgerton estate. Now, I bid you good evening, sir."

She turned to enter the house, and with a rush, he was at her side. He took her arm in a hard grip and began pulling her away from the door.

"Easy to say, miss – but I don't believe you. You've been sniffing about Edward Havens for years. Of course you want to try and solve his problems."

The shrubbery caught at her skirts, and Miranda pried at his fingers, apprehension prickling over her.

"I really don't – "

"No. Better if you had a little accident, I think. Took a misstep and tumbled into the ravine."

His words filled her with ice. "Mr. Fowler, there's no need for this. Unhand me, and I will simply return home and speak not a word."

He yanked her close and trapped her other arm, then began pushing her toward the edge of the garden. There was, indeed, a ravine there, a sudden chasm. It was bounded by tall hedges – but nothing that would keep a determined person out.

"Let go of me."

Her lungs tightened, her breath coming in gasps. Miranda dug in her heels and pulled at his hands, trying to free herself from his grip.

She could not believe this was happening – that the estate manager intended to throw her into the ravine. Such things occurred in lurid novels, perhaps, but not outside the pages of books.

Mr. Fowler leaned close. His breath smelled of onions and alcohol as he hissed into her ear, "It's for the best, Miss Price."

Full panic struck her then – the marrow-cold knowledge that she was in deep, deep trouble.

"Help!" she cried.

They were not that far from the walls of Edgerton Manor. Someone in the house must be able to hear – a servant or one of the guests. She drew in another breath, ready to scream again, but Mr. Fowler clamped a rough hand over her mouth, forcing her jaw closed.

"No more of that," he growled.

Miranda began to fight him in earnest, struggling and kicking. She clawed for his face, twisted, trying to aim her knee at his sensitive spot.

Cursing in an undertone, Mr. Fowler continued dragging her to the hedge. She could not breathe – his hand was covering her nose now. Bright spots flashed before her eyes.

The sharp spines of hawthorn pierced her gown and scraped her skin as Mr. Fowler thrust her into the hedge.

"A…little… further," he said, grunting with effort as he forced them both into the painful, wiry foliage.

Then they were through. Just ahead, the ground fell away. In the dim grey light, the ravine was a dark slash. Miranda's thoughts tangled desperately in her mind. The ravine was not treacherously deep. When Mr. Fowler pushed her over the edge, the fall would certainly cause her harm – but she did not think it would kill her.

Mr. Fowler paused, as if thinking the same thing.

"Miranda!" It was Edward's voice, calling from the shadows. "Where are you?"

She struggled against Mr. Fowler's hard grip, desperate to break free. Surely Edward could hear the thrashing in the shrubbery? He must.

Mr. Fowler lifted his hand from over her mouth and nose. Miranda drew in a deep breath.

"HEL – "

A sharp, crashing pain to her temple, and everything went black.

***

Edward slammed through the door and raced into the garden. Surely that had been Miranda's voice. He scanned the shadows – but no one was there. The plants lay quiescent, their blooms folded away. A cricket chirped from off to his right.

"Really, Edward," Leticia Davenport said, coming up behind him and curling her arm through his. "It was some night bird calling. Look, the garden is empty. In fact, the rose arbor is very romantic by night. Shall we go there, instead?"

He shook her off and strode forward, pulse hammering. "Go back into the house, and roust the footmen."

"Surely not."

"Go." He whirled on her and pointed back toward the tall brick wall of the manor.

"Why, I – "

"Shh." He waved her to silence. Had he heard something?

A rustling sound, from the far hedge. Perhaps some night creature – but he could not shake the sense of dread tightening about his ribs. Miranda was out here, and she was in trouble.

His mind flashed back to the curricle accident she and her brother had suffered. Upon retrieving the broken vehicle, his head groom had told him the axle break was odd. Edward had thought no more of it, but he should have at least considered if the curricle had been deliberately tampered with. Even in West Dorset there were villains.

Damnation, he should have paid closer attention all along.

"Miranda!" he called into the dark. "Where are you?"

The disturbance in the hedge increased, the hawthorn branches shivering violently. Edward sprinted toward it. Didn't the ravine lie beyond?

"HEL – "

The cry came from just ahead. He forced his way into the hedge, heedless of the sharp thorns tearing at him. In the dim light, he saw the figure of a man poised at the edge of the deep gully. And lying in a crumpled heap at his feet –

"Miranda," he said again, his heart clenching.

In three steps, he was on the man, pulling him away from where Miranda lay. He took a moment to register Fowler's surprised face before his fist connected with the man's jaw.

"Hoy!" Fowler cried, staggering back. "My lord, it's not what you think. She lured me out here, said – "

"Enough." Edward made a grab for his arm, but the man flung himself away.

A second later, Fowler flailed his arms, teetering for balance on the edge of the ravine. His eyes flashed, wide and panicked in the last bit of twilight seeping from the sky. Edward lunged, his fingers catching purchase on the man's coat, then slipping away as the estate manager tumbled down.

Fowler's yell reverberated, accompanied by the thumping echo of a body falling through brush and over stones. Edward checked the impulse to leap after him. Fowler could lay where he had fallen – he must tend to Miranda now.

Edward went to his knees and gently pulled her into his arms, relief a crashing wave over him as he found she was still warm, still breathing.

If he had lost her… he shook his head. What a blind idiot he'd been. The happiness he'd been foolishly pursuing in London had been here all along, under his nose, disguised as a lovely, bookish country miss.

He bent and brushed a kiss over her forehead, and Miranda moaned and stirred.

"Edward?" she said, a faint tremble in her voice.

"I'm here." He folded his arms around her, holding her firmly, gently.

"Good." She drew in a deep, shuddering breath. "The money – it was Fowler, all along."

"I gathered as much. But hush now. We must get you back to the manor. Can you stand?"

He did not relish pushing back through the hedge and exposing her to those sharp thorns, but if he went first, shielding her with his body, she should be protected.

"I think so," she said, taking a deep breath. "My head hurts, but I am otherwise unharmed."

"Steady now." Edward rose, drawing her up with him,

then pulled her once more into the shelter of his arms.

Behind the hedge, he heard raised voices. Had Leticia Davenport shown a modicum of sense for once, and actually gone to fetch help? Squaring his shoulders, Edward backed into the hawthorn. An uncomfortable moment later, he and Miranda emerged into the gardens.

Lantern-light hit his eyes, making him blink as a small crowd rushed toward them.

"Edward! Miranda – what the devil happened?" Charlie asked.

"Fowler. He's back in the ravine." Edward tilted his head to the hedge, but his arms were occupied, still wrapped around Miranda.

He didn't care what the onlookers thought. That ring in his pocket was going to serve a purpose tonight. Provided Miranda would have him. The fact that she did not protest his embrace was a good sign.

"I'll see to him," Charlie said.

His lips folded into a grim line, and he beckoned two of the burlier footmen to accompany him.

"My dear girl!" Miranda's mother hurried forward. "I'm so worried for you. Are you well?"

She gave Edward a sharp look, and he reluctantly let Miranda go. She sighed as she stepped out of his arms.

"I am well enough, mother."

"You're shivering," Mrs. Price said.

"Everyone, come back into the house," Lady Edgerton said. "Edward and Miranda can tell us what occurred, but they deserve to be comfortable while they do so."

Leticia Davenport sniffed at the words, and Edward caught her sending a glare full of blades in Miranda's direction.

"It was lucky that Edward and I were in the study together," Leticia said. "Alone. When we heard Miss Price cry out."

Damn the girl. She seemed determined to wring a proposal out of him yet.

"Fortunate that you came upon me there," he said, "and a moment later could fetch help while I went in search of Miranda."

"Inside," his mother said, gesturing.

"One moment." Edward held up his hand. "I want to make something perfectly clear. There was to be a betrothal tonight."

The onlookers quieted, and Leticia leaned forward, her eyes gleaming in the lantern light.

He slipped his fingers into his coat pocket. Miraculously, the engagement ring was still there. He drew it out and held it up, the faceted diamonds winking. Leticia wet her lips.

"Isn't this a bit public, darling?" his mother asked.

"It must be done now," he said.

There would be too many innuendos, too much maneuvering, if he did not deal with matters directly. He would not let his chance, his heart slip away into the night.

Leticia Davenport stepped up, a calculating smile on her face. "Oh, Edward, if you would like to wait, you may be sure of my answer."

"It's not your answer I need," he said.

He turned toward Miranda, where she stood in the shelter of her mother's arm. Her face was pale and strained, unhappiness shading her expression. Did she truly still think he was planning to offer for Miss Davenport?

Edward went down on one knee, uncaring of the scratches on his skin, the bruises on his knuckles where he had hit Mr. Fowler. None of that was important – only the widening of Miranda's eyes as he took her scraped hand in his.

"Miss Miranda Price," he said. "Would you do me the very great honor of becoming my wife?"

He scarcely heard Leticia Davenport's strangled protest over the thudding of his heart as he stared up into Miranda's eyes. Everything hung upon this moment.

The lamplight shone steady and golden around them, and the faint fragrance of roses tickled his nose. His knee was damp. Overhead, the first stars sprinkled across the sky.

He had never felt more alive in his life.

Miranda swallowed, and Edward held his breath. His whole body vibrated with a single question.

Then a sweetness came into her face, a tenderness about her lips, and he knew he was saved.

"Yes," she said.

The syllable resonated through him. Quickly, before she could change her mind, he slipped the ring onto her finger.

"Huzzah!" It was Charlie, who had returned with leaves in his hair and a satisfied light in his eyes. "High time, too. I was beginning to fear you'd take the wrong path altogether. My deepest congratulations to you both."

Miranda looked at Edward, an expression of pure happiness suffusing her features. She used to look like that, he recalled – years ago. Carefree and full of the joy of life.

Beside her, her mother beamed. Edward rose and turned to his own mother, a kernel of worry in his chest. It was not the outcome she had been expecting.

Still, her smile seemed genuine. "I am pleased for you,"

she said.

"Well, I am not," said Leticia Davenport in a shrill voice. "How could you behave in such a dishonorable fashion? It is simply beyond me. Come mother. I cannot bear to stay here another instant."

She turned on her heel and stalked away, her exit marred by the fact that she had no lantern and stumbled into a few bushes before she found the door.

Lady Davenport gave Edward's mother a look. "Ah, children. They always do what they will, not what we want for them."

"And isn't that for the best?" Lady Edgerton said.

"You're not disappointed?" Edward asked his mother in a low voice.

"How could I be, when you are clearly so happy?" She gave his cheek a gentle pat. "Now, go help escort your betrothed home. Heavens, we have so much planning to do!"

***

In light of Fowler's actions, Edward insisted the Price family return home in his carriage, rather than their own vehicle. He promised to have his footmen inspect it carefully for signs of tampering and deliver it on the morrow.

As the carriage turned toward Wyckerly, Miranda rested her head against Edward's shoulder. The oil lamps let off a faintly pungent scent and the dark blue curtains shut out the night. Her mother and Charlie occupied the bench across from them, and Mother did not seem to think it improper that the earl had his arm around Miranda's shoulders.

It did not feel improper – it felt deliciously comforting.

The ride home had been full of talk about the events of the evening, although she had mostly remained quiet. Her head still pounded at intervals, and she could not quite believe all that had happened – despite the evidence of the ring on her finger. And the even-more-convincing proof of Edward's arm about her.

Charlie had described finding Fowler partway down the ravine, his leg twisted beneath him. The footmen had taken him to the local magistrate, where he was currently locked up.

"It's a fair guess he was embezzling heavily from the estate," Charlie said. "Miranda must have been getting too close to uncovering his secrets."

"The old ledger," she said. "He was keeping double-books, and using the older account ledgers to work out how he was going to move and hide the money – I'm sure of it. And I think he sold off one of the smaller holdings, as well."

Edward pressed her hand. "We'll find the evidence, and the money, thanks to you. I only wish involving you in the estate's business hadn't proved so perilous."

"On the other hand," Charlie said, "it saved you from marrying Leticia Davenport, so my sister's peril was worth it."

"Now, Charles," their mother said, "be kind."

Whether she meant to herself or to Miss Davenport, Miranda wasn't sure. Or perhaps to Edward, who still had a wild-eyed look.

The carriage slowed as they turned into Wyckerly's drive. Miranda's mother gathered her reticule and looked at Charlie.

"We'll go in, and give the happy couple a moment alone, shall we?"

Charlie's brows rose, and he glanced across at Edward. "Be good to my sister, Edgerton."

"Without question, Price."

"And you," Charlie turned his gaze on Miranda. "Keep him in order. I'd hate to be forced to challenge him to a duel before the wedding day dawns."

She felt a blush heating her cheeks. "As long as fruit is your weapon of choice," she said. "But I assure you, I can manage the earl."

Though she was not at all certain that she could.

Beside her, Edward chuckled – an astonishingly dear sound to her ears.

The driver swung open the carriage door, and Miranda's family exited. The door closed quietly behind them. She was a bit shocked that her mother so easily colluded to give them a moment alone. Had everyone but herself and Edward thought they would suit as a couple? The notion left her breathless.

In the quiet warmth of the carriage, Miranda was suddenly, dazzlingly aware of Edward's solid presence next to her. The Earl of Edgerton had asked her to marry him!

Had the knock to her head made her take leave of her senses, so that she believed all her vain dreams had become reality? But no, Edward was there, gazing at her with eyes darkened by emotion. The light teased golden glints from his hair, shone on the strong planes of his face.

"Miranda," he said.

Only her name, but it was enough. Her heart opened like a flower unfurling. She turned and slid her hands about his neck, pulling him close. The scent of musk mingled with the night air, and he dipped his head. Their mouths met, heat and hunger and apology all at once.

She parted her lips and let her tongue touch his. Sparks raced along her nerves at the delicious, forbidden contact. His hands stroked down her arms and skimmed along her sides, brushing the curves of her breasts. Fire sprang up inside her, a sudden, insistent flame kindled at her center. She pressed herself more closely to his broad chest, felt, more than heard, his groan of desire.

His thumb coasted over the peak of her breast, and she gasped.

"Wicked man," she managed, through lips tingling with the imprint of his kiss.

"Mm." He drew back and smiled at her, a lazy, roguish smile. "My lady, you've no idea."

She gently scraped her fingernails down the sides of his neck. "I expect I'll learn."

Passion flared in his eyes, and he took her mouth again in a kiss that seared her to her soul. In a moment, they must pull apart, their two bodies un-melding, but for now she savored every second. The firmness of his muscled chest, beneath his linen shirt and fine waistcoat, his arms hard about her, the demands of his mouth as he swept his tongue in to taste her – she drank him in. She suspected she would never be quenched.

But the driver was knocking, respectfully yet firmly, at the carriage door. With a sigh, Miranda pulled away.

"I think," she said, "marriage to you is going to be wonderful, Lord Edgerton."

He gave her a smile that surely had sent the London ladies swooning. "I have every intention of making it so."

A pity she had to wait a little longer to wed the earl. Both their mothers insisted on doing things properly – which would mean an extensive guest list and more details than she wanted to contemplate. Stifling a sigh, Miranda let Edward assist her from the carriage. Then, hand in hand, they ascended the stairs of Wyckerly. Just outside the doors, he paused.

"I believe I've neglected to mention a few items of importance." The lilt in his voice told her she had nothing to fear.

"Oh?"

He took both her hands. "I find you very attractive. I admire your mind. You are welcome in my business, and in my life. In short, Miss Miranda Price, though I should have mentioned it earlier, I love you."

She stared up into his face, tears dazzling the corners of her eyes.

"Despite the fact you are reputedly a scoundrel," she said, "I confess I love you in return."

"Perhaps you might like to add that to the pages of your diary," he said, a teasing tilt to his lips. "Just so there's no confusion."

At that, she laughed. The night breeze fluttered her skirts, Edward's hands were warm over hers, and the sweet smell of some dark-blooming flower suffused the air. Her soul shivered, like a wild bird freed, then took flight, soaring into the perfect, star-bedecked sky.

~THE END~

Other Titles by Anthea Lawson

Passionate – A finalist for the prestigious RWA RITA award, this Victorian-set novel takes the reader on a romantic adventure from the ballrooms and parlors of London through the Mediterranean to the exotic valleys of Tunisia. Fans of Julia Quinn and Connie Brockway will enjoy this witty foray into the outer edges of civilization — and propriety.

"A lush, exotic tale of romance and adventure." – Sally MacKenzie, USA Today bestselling author

All He Desires – Self-exiled on the Isle of Crete, an English doctor with a troubled past meets the one woman who can bring him out of the shadows and into the light.

"Lawson, a RITA-nominated husband-and-wife writing team, deftly combines danger, desire, and a deliciously different Victorian setting into a sexy version of Victoria Holt's classic gothic romances." – Booklist Reviews

Visit Anthea's website at www.anthealawson.com, friend her on Facebook, follow her on Twitter. See you there~

About the Author

Anthea Lawson's first two novels were co-written by Anthea and Lawson, a husband and wife creative team living in the Pacific Northwest. Their first novel, *Passionate,* was released from Kensington books in October 2008, and was a nominee for the prestigious RWA RITA award for Best First Book.

Since 2010, Anthea has branched out solo, continuing to write historical romance, as well as Young Adult Urban Fantasy as Anthea Sharp. Anthea is still happily married and living in the Northwest with her husband and daughter, where the rainy days and excellent coffee fuel her writing.

In addition to writing, Anthea and Lawson play traditional Celtic music in the band Fiddlehead. Hear samples of their music at www.cdbaby.com/Artist/Fiddlehead.

Made in the USA
Middletown, DE
15 January 2026